THE SpongeBob SquarePants MOVIE™

NICKELODEON®

by Marc Cerasini

SCHOLASTIC INC.

New York   Toronto   London   Auckland   Sydney
Mexico City   New Delhi   Hong Kong   Buenos Aires

Stephen Hillenburg

Based on the *The SpongeBob SquarePants Movie* by Nickelodeon Movies and Paramount Pictures

ISBN 0-439-66693-7

12 11 10 9 8 7 6 5 4 3 2 1   4 5 6 7 8 9/0

Printed in the U.S.A.   40

First Scholastic printing, November 2004

CHAPTER 1

We begin our story under calm blue waters, near the beautiful green island of Bikini Atoll. Beneath those tropical seas we find the town of Bikini Bottom, a peaceful place where everyone is happy and—

Wait a minute! Hold your sea horses!

Things were *usually* happy in Bikini Bottom, but on this day, there was panic in the streets. Sirens wailed and frightened fish swam in all directions. Police helicopters buzzed over the town and squad cars blocked the intersections. The situation was so bad that classes at the school of fish were canceled!

In front of the Krusty Krab restaurant, a crowd had gathered. Mr. Krabs, the owner, was talking to reporters. They clustered around, waving microphones under his nose and pressing cameras into his face.

"Can you tell us what is happening, Mr. Krabs?" asked a young reporter from the *Daily Clam*.

"Wait! Please settle down," said Mr. Krabs, waving his claws. "One question at a time. Please! One at a time!"

"The people of Bikini Bottom want to know—what's going on inside?" asked Perch Perkins, Bikini Bottom's favorite newsman.

"We've got a situation in there that I'd rather not talk about until my manager gets here."

Suddenly a sleek black sports car pulled up to the curb.

"Look!" cried Mr. Krabs. "There he is!"

All eyes—and eyestalks—turned to see SpongeBob SquarePants step out of the black car. His face was somber, his eyes hidden behind sunglasses. In his hand the determined sponge carried an important-looking briefcase.

"It's SquarePants!" a fish cried out in a voice filled with awe.

SpongeBob walked right up to Mr. Krabs and tore off his sunglasses.

"Talk to me, Krabs," he said in a commanding voice.

"It started out as a simple order," Mr. Krabs sobbed. "A Krabby Patty with cheese."

"So what went wrong?" asked SpongeBob.

"When the customer took a bite,"—Mr. Krabs choked and continued to sob—"there was no cheese!" Mr. Krabs cried. "No *cheese* on the sandwich. This has never happened before."

Mr. Krabs broke down. He covered his eyestalks with his claws and sobbed. SpongeBob slapped him on the snout.

"Get ahold of yourself, Eugene," said SpongeBob. "I'm going in."

Mr. Krabs stopped crying and sighed with relief.

SpongeBob turned and faced the restaurant. Reporters and innocent bystanders backed away under his stern gaze. The crowd parted to make a path for him—a path that led to the front door of the Krusty Krab.

SpongeBob boldly entered the restaurant. The dining room was deserted, except for one very frightened fish sitting alone at a table. On a tray in front of him sat a Krabby Patty with a single bite missing.

Fearlessly SpongeBob SquarePants walked over to the anxious fish.

"Who . . . who are you?" the fish asked in a shaky voice.

"I'm the manager of this establishment," replied SpongeBob in a businesslike tone.

Then SpongeBob slapped his briefcase down on the table. The nervous fish jumped at the sound.

"Everything is gonna be fine," SpongeBob said in a calm voice.

But the poor fish just shook his head. "I'm really scared, man."

"You got a name?"

The fish nodded. "Phil."

"You got a family, Phil?"

The fish got choked up, then began to cry.

SpongeBob snapped his fingers in front of Phil's face.

"Come on, Phil! Stay with me. Let's hear about that family."

"I . . . I got a lovely wife and two beautiful children," Phil stammered.

"That's what it's all about, Phil," SpongeBob replied.

As Phil watched nervously, SpongeBob reached into his briefcase. Then he looked up at Phil.

"I've only got one shot at this," SpongeBob warned. "Gotta have the right tools for the job. . . ."

SpongeBob paused, rifling through his briefcase. Then he looked up and whispered, "Bingo!" Slowly, he pulled out a pair of shiny, golden tongs.

"Now I want you to do me a favor, Phil," SpongeBob said.

"Wh-what?" the fish gasped.

"Say *cheese!*"

With that, SpongeBob placed a perfectly cut slice of yellow cheese in the center of the bun. Then he looked up into Phil's grateful, smiling face.

Success!

Minutes later SpongeBob came out of the Krusty

Krab's front door, looking pleased with himself. He carried Phil safely in his arms.

"Order up!" SpongeBob said. Customers cheered and flocked to fill the tables.

SpongeBob was lifted into the air and carried through town on the crowd's shoulders. All around him, confetti fluttered down like snow.

"Three cheers for the manager!" they cried. "Hip, hip—HONK!"

"What?" SpongeBob said sleepily.

"Hip, hip—HONK!"

And just like that, the dream was over. SpongeBob SquarePants sat up in his bed and blinked his eyes.

"HONK!"

He turned off his alarm clock before it honked again.

"Hooray!" SpongeBob cried, throwing off his blanket. "Gary! I had that dream again. And it's finally going to come true. Today!"

He raced over to the calendar.

"Sorry about this, calendar," SpongeBob said as he tore away yesterday's page. The date underneath on the calendar read MARCH 7.

SpongeBob stepped back and admired the calendar.

"Today is the grand opening ceremony of the Krusty Krab 2, where Mr. Krabs is going to announce the new manager."

"Meow," said Gary, and the little snail slid over to SpongeBob's side.

"Who's it gonna be, Gary?" said SpongeBob. Then he got an idea.

"I know. Why don't we ask my wall of three hundred seventy-four consecutive Employee of the Month Awards?"

"SpongeBob SquarePants!" yelled all 374 pictures of SpongeBob on the wall.

"Hooray for me!" said SpongeBob as he ran to the bathroom to get ready for work. While he showered he sang.

"I'm ready. Promotion! I'm ready. Promotion!"

In the shower SpongeBob took the paper off a bar of soap and ate the whole bar of soap. Then he soaked water up until he was so inflated he could hardly fit in the bathroom.

Holding his nose and closing his mouth, SpongeBob made two fists and strained. Bubbles and water poured out of his sponge holes. Soon SpongeBob was back to normal size—and clean as a whistle!

Still thrilled about his soon-to-be promotion, SpongeBob danced over to the closet. He searched until he found the perfect square pants for this special day, the same square shorts and shirt he always wore.

When he was dressed, SpongeBob ran back to the bathroom. He pulled down the brush and squeezed the tube of toothpaste. SpongeBob brushed his teeth, then his ears, and then his eyeballs, until they sparkled. SpongeBob admired his reflection in the mirror. "Cleanliness is next to managerliness," he declared.

Then the happy sponge gave little Gary his breakfast and skipped off to work. As he went, SpongeBob was still singing.

"I'm ready. Promotion! I'm ready. Promotion!"

He sang until he got to Squidward's house, right next door. Without bothering to knock, SpongeBob opened the door and walked right in!

CHAPTER 2

Squidward was enjoying the only thing he *did* enjoy on a workday—his morning shower. As he lathered up, he hummed a song.

"Doo, doo, doo . . . doo, dee, dee, dee . . ."

Suddenly Squidward felt a hand on his back. He opened one eye to see SpongeBob standing next to him in the shower.

"SpongeBob! What are you doing in here?"

SpongeBob grinned. "I have to tell you something, Squidward."

But Squidward wasn't in the mood to listen. "Whatever it is, can't it wait until work?"

"There's no shower at work," SpongeBob replied.

Squidward wiped the soap out of his eyes. He

was getting angrier by the minute. "What do you want?"

"I just wanted to say I'll be thanking you in my managerial acceptance speech today," said SpongeBob.

Squidward replied by throwing SpongeBob out of his house. SpongeBob flew through the air and landed with a loud squish next to a big rock.

The rock popped up—and there was Patrick stuck to the bottom.

"That sounds like the manager of the new Krusty Krab 2," said Patrick in his sweet, dopey voice. "Congratulations, buddy!"

Patrick gave SpongeBob a high five.

"Oh thanks, Patrick," SpongeBob replied. "And tonight after my big promotion we're gonna party till we're purple!"

Patrick clapped. "I love being purple."

"We're going to the place where all the action is," said SpongeBob.

Patrick's eyes bugged out. "You don't mean—"

"Yes, Patrick, I mean—the Goofy Goober's Party Boat!" cried SpongeBob.

Patrick clapped so hard, the rock came down and squashed them both. When it popped up again, SpongeBob and Patrick were both wearing their favorite headgear: peanut-shaped Goofy Goober hats!

"I'm a Goofy Goober, yeah!" sang SpongeBob.

Patrick sang back, "You're a Goofy Goober, yeah!"

Then they put their heads together. "We're all Goofy Goobers, yeah! Goofy, Goofy, Goober, Goober, yeah!"

Then SpongeBob glanced at his watch and gasped. "I'd better get going!"

SpongeBob pulled off his Goofy Goober hat.

"Bye, Patrick. I don't want to be late for my big promotion."

"Good luck, SpongeBob," said Patrick.

As he ran down the sidewalk to the Krusty Krab, SpongeBob broke into his shower song again.

"I'm ready! Promotion. I'm ready! Promotion!"

"Hey!" Patrick called. "Look for me at the ceremony. I've got a little surprise for you."

Meanwhile the excitement was building at the Krusty Krab. The whole place was decorated with balloons. There was a big banner that read GRAND OPENING. And right next to the restaurant was a big tent.

Inside the Krusty Krab, residents of Bikini Bottom crowded around a big stage. And standing onstage was everybody's favorite newsman. He was talking in front of a television camera.

"Hello, Bikini Bottom. Perch Perkins here, coming to you live from inside the Krusty Krab restaurant."

The news anchor smiled into the camera. His teeth sparkled.

"For years this was the only place to get a delicious and mouthwatering Krabby Patty—until today, that is!"

Everybody cheered.

"That's right, folks. Longtime owner, Mr. Krabs, is opening a new restaurant called the Krusty Krab 2," said Perch Perkins as Mr. Krabs walked onto the stage, waving to the crowd.

The huge tent was pulled off the building next to the Krusty Krab, and there stood the Krusty Krab 2. It looked exactly the same as the original restaurant, and it was right next door!

Everybody cheered again.

"First of all, congratulations, Mr. Krabs," said Perch Perkins.

Mr. Krabs stepped up to the microphone. "Hello," he said. "I like money."

"So tell us, Mr. Krabs, what inspired you to build a second Krab restaurant right next door to the original?" Perch Perkins asked.

"Money."

But not *everybody* was happy. It was a very different scene at Plankton's restaurant, the Chum Bucket, across the street.

The place was a gloomy little shack with walls that needed painting and tables that wobbled. As usual, the Chum Bucket was empty.

Plankton, the teeny-eensie-weensie owner (and longtime enemy of Mr. Krabs), stood at the window.

He was watching the opening ceremony at Krusty Krab 2 through a long telescope.

"Curses," Plankton cried. "It's not fair. Not fair at all! Krabs is being interviewed by Perch Perkins and I've never had even one customer."

Plankton got so angry that the big vein on the back of his head nearly exploded.

"Don't get all worked up again, Plankton. I just mopped the floors," said Karen the Computer, his wife.

Plankton shook his head sadly.

"Oh, Karen, my computer wife," he sighed. "If only I could have managed to steal the secret to Krabs's success—the formula for the delicious Krabby Patty."

Plankton wanted the secret formula so much that he imagined the bottle was floating over his head. He tried to reach for the bottle. But it faded away before his eyes.

"Ahhhhh!" Plankton screamed. He began to pace across the room, back and forth.

"Ohh, if I had that secret formula, then people

would line up to eat at my restaurant. Lord knows I've tried."

As he spoke Plankton moved to the back of the restaurant, where his Evil Laboratory was hidden.

Inside the Evil Laboratory energy crackled from huge metal rods and chemicals bubbled in big beakers. On the wall hundreds of bottles were lined up. Each bottle was marked:

FAILURE NUMBER 87

MISERABLE FAILURE NUMBER 190

REALLY TRAGIC AND HORRIBLE FAILURE NUMBER 262

Plankton ignored the equipment and the bottles. He walked over to a big metal cabinet and opened the bottom drawer.

"I've exhausted every evil plan in my filing cabinet, from *A* to *Y*."

"*A* to *Y*?" said Karen the Computer.

"Yeah," Plankton replied. "*A* to *Y*. You know, the alphabet?"

"What about *Z*?"

"*Z*?"

"*Z*," Karen said. "The letter that comes after *Y*."

Plankton scratched his head. Then he flipped through his files. "*W . . . X . . . Y . . .*"

He froze.

"And *Z*!"

Plankton pulled out a thick folder marked with a big *Z*.

"Plan Z!" he said triumphantly. "Here it is. Just like you said!"

Karen the Computer rolled her eyes. "Oh, boy."

Plankton gloated as he flipped through the pages, reading all about Plan Z. When he was finished, he hopped around the Evil Laboratory. He was so happy, he was practically giddy.

"Ohhh . . . it's evil," sang Plankton. "It's . . . it's . . . diabolical!" He stuck his nose in the folder and sniffed. "And it's lemon scented! This plan has got it all!"

When Plankton closed the folder, his eyes glowed with an evil light.

"This Plan Z can't possibly fail!" he exclaimed.

"Where have I heard *that* before?" said Karen the Computer with a sigh.

But Plankton was too excited to hear Karen. He left the Evil Laboratory and slid through the dining room.

"So enjoy today, Mr. Krabs," Plankton cried, "because by tomorrow *I'll* have the formula. Then everyone will eat at the Chum Bucket, and *I* will rule the world!"

Plankton slid out the front door and shook his fist at the people of Bikini Bottom.

"All hail Plankton! All hail—"

Then a giant foot came down on Plankton's head and squashed him flat, like he was nothing more than . . . well, plankton.

CHAPTER 3

The giant black shoe that Plankton was stuck to the bottom of belonged to SpongeBob SquarePants. He was on his way to work and he was still singing the promotion song.

But when he heard the squish—and Plankton's cries of pain—SpongeBob stopped.

"Ew," he said. "I think I stepped in something."

SpongeBob slammed his foot down and wiped it on the ground.

"Aaaaaaaaaarrrggghhh!" howled Plankton.

"Get . . . off . . . of . . . my . . . shoe," grunted SpongeBob, wiping again.

"Aaaaaaaaaarrrggghhh!"

"I stepped in something gross. Now it won't

come off," said SpongeBob.

"Not *in* something. *On* something, you twit!" yelled Plankton angrily.

SpongeBob lifted his shoe and saw Plankton stuck to the bottom.

"Oh, sorry, Plankton."

SpongeBob reached down and peeled Plankton off his shoe.

"Owwww!"

"Are you on your way to the grand opening ceremony?" SpongeBob asked.

"No, I am not on my way to the grand opening ceremony," Plankton sneered. "I'm busy planning TO RULE THE WORLD!"

Then Plankton laughed maniacally.

SpongeBob stared at him, blinked twice, and said, "Well, good luck with that."

Then SpongeBob skipped away and continued singing. "I'm ready! Promotion. I'm ready! Promotion."

Plankton watched him go and just shook his head. "Stupid kid."

When SpongeBob reached the Krusty Krab 2, he couldn't believe his eyes. Everyone who was anyone was there. It was a real show! The new Krusty Krab 2 restaurant was just as cool as the original. Even better, it was right next door.

"That Mr. Krabs is a genius," said SpongeBob. "No wonder he makes so much money."

"Welcome," said Mr. Krabs. "Welcome, everyone, to the grand opening of the Krusty Krab 2."

Mrs. Puff inflated her puffer belly and scowled. She turned to Sandy Cheeks. "I can't believe we paid nine dollars for this!" she said.

"I paid ten!" said Sandy.

As SpongeBob pushed his way to the front of the crowd, he spied Mr. Krabs. The proud owner had his claws raised. He was almost ready to cut the ceremonial ribbon and officially open the new restaurant.

"Before we begin with the ribbon cutting, I'd like to introduce our new manager."

"Yes!" shouted SpongeBob as he danced in a circle. "Yeah! Now we're talkin'!"

Squidward, sitting next to SpongeBob, sighed,

hoping this would all be over soon.

"Ahem . . . well, anyway," Mr. Krabs began. "The new manager is a loyal, hardworking employee . . ."

"Yes!" said SpongeBob, sticking his thumb into his chest.

". . . and the obvious choice for the job," said Mr. Krabs.

SpongeBob looked up at Squidward. "He's right!"

"And it is a name you all know—a name that starts with an *S*."

"That's me!" crowed SpongeBob.

Mr. Krabs rolled his eyes, then continued. "Please welcome our new area manager . . . Squidward Tentacles!"

Behind Mr. Krabs, a huge banner with Squidward's face on it was lowered from the ceiling. Another banner unrolled below. It read CONGRATULATIONS, SQUIDWARD.

"Yes! Yes!" screamed SpongeBob, jumping up and down like a crazy sponge. Then he turned to Squidward.

"Better luck next time, buddy," said SpongeBob. "Wooooo-hooo!"

SpongeBob leaped onto the stage and knocked Mr. Krabs aside.

"Yeah! All right! Hooray for me!" cried SpongeBob.

In front of everyone, SpongeBob spoke into the microphone.

"People of Bikini Bottom, as the manager—"

"Ah, SpongeBob," said Mr. Krabs, tapping him on the shoulder.

"Hold the phone, folks," said SpongeBob. "I'm getting an important news flash from Mr. Krabs. Manager stuff. Go ahead, Mr. K.!"

Mr. Krabs leaned in and whispered something in SpongeBob's ear. SpongeBob listened, then spoke right into the microphone. "I'm making a complete *what* out of myself?"

Mr. Krabs cringed and whispered some more.

"The most embarrassing thing you've ever seen?" repeated SpongeBob loudly.

Mr. Krabs whispered again.

SpongeBob looked confused. "And now it's worse because I'm repeating everything you say into the microphone?"

"Oh, for crying out loud, SpongeBob!" Krabs yelled at last. "You didn't get the job."

SpongeBob's jaw dropped and his eyes got wet. He couldn't believe his ears.

"What . . . ?" he squeaked.

Mr. Krabs repeated, "You. Did not. Get. The job."

SpongeBob's heart sank. "But . . . but why?"

Mr. Krabs put his arm around SpongeBob's shoulders. "SpongeBob, you're a great fry cook, but I gave the job to Squidward because being manager is a big responsibility, and . . . well . . . let's face it—he's more mature than you."

SpongeBob looked up at Mr. Krabs with sad eyes. "I'm not mature?"

"Oh, lad," said Mr. Krabs. "I mean this in the nicest of ways. But, well, there's a word for what you are . . . er . . . ah . . ."

But Mr. Krabs couldn't remember the word, so the crowd helped out.

"Dork?" a fish called.

Mr. Krabs shook his head. "No, wait. . . . That's not right. Not dork . . ."

"A goofball," said Pearl, Mr. Krabs's daughter.

"Closer, but no," Mr. Krabs replied.

"A ding-a-ling?" cried someone else.

"Wing nut!"

"A Knucklehead McSpazatron!" yelled an old lady.

With each insult SpongeBob became more depressed.

"Okay, that's enough!" Mr. Krabs commanded. Then he patted SpongeBob on the back.

"Look, what I am trying to say is you're just a kid. And to be a manager you have to be a man. Otherwise, they'd call it a *kidager*. You understandager—I mean, do you understand, SpongeBob?"

"I guess so, Mr. Krabs," mumbled SpongeBob. Heartbroken, SpongeBob climbed off the stage. As he trudged away Mr. Krabs called him, but SpongeBob couldn't hear anything. He was too sad.

"I'm ready. Depression," sang SpongeBob with a sigh. "I'm ready. . . . Depression."

Mr. Krabs shook his head sadly. "Poor kid."

Suddenly someone shouted, "Hooray for SpongeBob!"

Everyone looked up to see Patrick swing down from the sky. SpongeBob's best starfish friend was dressed in balloons and dragging a big banner that read HOORAY FOR SPONGEBOB.

Patrick slammed right into the giant Squirdward banner, sending the whole stage crashing to the ground. The crowd scattered in panic. From inside the middle of the wreckage, Patrick's dopey, sweet voice called out.

"Where did everybody go?"

CHAPTER 4

Later that evening, while the good citizens of Bikini Bottom slept in their beds, Plankton launched his evil plan. Using a helicopter jet pack, he took off and flew through the night. When he saw his final destination, he began to chuckle to himself. "Heh, heh, heh, heh! It's time to put Plan Z into effect."

Plankton landed on a dark hill. He turned off his jet pack. Then he stared out at the beautiful castle of seashells and pearls in front of him.

"My evil plan starts right here, at the undersea castle of King Neptune!" Plankton said to himself.

Chuckling with glee, he floated up to the castle's biggest window and peeked inside.

On his giant throne sat the great merman King Neptune. Neptune, the king of the sea, had a long beard and a big fish tail. He held his mighty trident in one hand, and on his head sat his golden crown.

To Plankton, the king seemed enormous!

Next to the huge king was his little daughter, Mindy. She was a very pretty mermaid with big eyes and a bright smile.

Just then the squire entered and blew his horn. Then he unrolled a scroll and read from it. "Royal court is now in session," announced the squire. "Will the prisoner step forward."

Two tough-looking guards entered. The guards carried in a defeated-looking fish, bound in fin-cuffs. "Sooooo," Neptune began. "You confess to the crime of touching the king's crown?"

"Yes, but . . . ," squeaked the fish.

"But what?" yelled King Neptune.

"But it's my job, Your Highness," the little fish replied. "I'm the royal crown polisher."

"Well," said King Neptune with a frown. "I guess that means I can't have you fried. So twenty years in the dungeon it is."

"Daddy!" cried Mindy, horrified.

She swam over to the fish and unlocked his fin-cuffs. The fish bowed politely.

"Thank you, Princess Mindy," said the royal polisher.

Then the little fish ran away as fast as he could. It was time for the royal polisher to find a new job.

"Mindy!" King Neptune roared. "How can you defy me?"

"But, Daddy! Why do you have to be so mean?"

"I am the king!" said Neptune, pounding his royal trident on the floor. "I must enforce the laws of the sea."

"Well, I wish you'd try some love and compassion instead of these harsh punishments," said Mindy.

"That would be nice," added the squire.

The king bonked the squire on the head with his trident.

"Squire! Clear the room," demanded Neptune. "I wish to speak with my daughter alone."

King Neptune reached up and pulled off the heavy crown, revealing his shiny bald head. Then he showed it to his daughter.

"What is this, Mindy?" asked the king.

"Your crown?" asked Mindy uncertainly.

"And what does this crown do, Mindy?" asked Neptune.

Mindy thought about it.

"Covers your bald spot?" she guessed.

"It's not bald!" the king bellowed defensively. "It's thinning. Thinning!"

After Neptune calmed down, he set his crown on the royal pillow and leaned forward.

"This crown does much more than cover a slightly receding hairline," said the king. "This crown entitles the one who wears it to be in charge of the sea."

While the king imparted some wisdom on his daughter, Plankton crept into the room. He tip-toed up to the pillow. Then, with a wicked chuckle, Plankton snatched the crown and slipped away without anyone noticing!

"One day you will wear this crown," continued King Neptune.

Mindy was horrified. "I'm gonna be bald!"

"Thinning!" Neptune cried. "But the point is you

won't be wearing it until you've learned how to rule with an iron fist, just like your father."

King Neptune reached for his crown. His hand grabbed the royal pillow instead. He placed the pillow on his head.

"Uh, Dad, your"—Mindy stopped and stared— "crown," she said, pointing.

With the pillow drooping over his ears, Neptune picked up a gilded hand mirror and gazed into it.

"What the——!" he yelled.

He frantically looked around the throne room, but the crown was gone. "My crown!" Neptune shouted.

Then he jumped up from his throne and roared with anger. The king howled and howled like a kid who just had his favorite toy taken away from him.

"Someone's stolen the royal crown! Guards! Mindy! Heeeeelllllp meeeeeee!"

<hr>

Meanwhile Plankton flew from the castle with his helicopter jet pack, carrying Neptune's crown and laughing to himself. As he flew back to Bikini Bottom, he passed over Goofy Goober's Party Boat!

The joint was rocking, and the music was blasting. A crowd of young fish were chowing down on delicious Goofy Goober's Ice-Cream Treats. The staff was rushing from table to table, delivering towers of ice cream.

There was ice cream covered with gobs of chocolate and piles of whipped cream. Ice cream with sprinkles, nuts, cherry, strawberry, or seaweed toppings. And huge banana splits with up to five flavors of ice cream and two big bananas.

And in the middle of all the fun and eating came an announcement. "Hey, all you Goobers! It's time to say *Hooowdy* to your favorite undersea peanut!"

Then the curtains parted and Goofy Goober—a large mechanical peanut—danced out in all of his peanut glory.

"Howdy, Goofy Goober!" all the fish cried.

Goofy Goober tipped his peanut hat and tapped his toes. "Hey, fellow Goofy Goobers," he said. "It's time to sing."

And as he did, the audience cheered!

"Oh, I'm a Goofy Goober, yeah!" he sang.

"Yeah!" shouted all the little fishes.

"You're a Goofy Goober, yeah!"

"Yeah!"

"Goofy, Goofy, Goober, Goober, yeah!"

Everyone was singing and scarfing down ice cream and having a good time.

Well, *almost* everyone.

At the ice-cream bar, one sad little sponge sat alone, crying in his soda.

"All right, get it together, old boy," SpongeBob told himself. Then he got a brilliant idea.

"I know. I'll just stop thinking about it."

SpongeBob stared at nothing for a long time.

"Hey, you know, I actually feel a little better," he said with a smile. "I don't even remember why I was sad."

Just then Patrick arrived. The starfish sat down next to SpongeBob at the bar.

"Heeey," said Patrick. "It's the new Krusty Krab 2 manager."

SpongeBob burst into tears.

"Wow. The pressure's already setting in," said Patrick.

"No, Patrick, you don't understand," SpongeBob said. "I didn't get the promotion."

Patrick was shocked. "What? Why?"

"Mr. Krabs thinks I'm a kid," said SpongeBob.

"What?" Patrick cried, slapping his head. "That's insane."

"I know," said SpongeBob.

"Well, saying you're a kid is . . . is like saying I'm a kid," said Patrick.

"Exactly," said SpongeBob.

The waiter set a tray in front of Patrick and said, "Here's your Goober Meal, sir."

"Hey," said Patrick suspiciously. "I'm supposed to get a toy with this."

The waiter tossed Patrick a stuffed peanut.

"Thanks!" said Patrick, cuddling it.

SpongeBob sighed. "I'm going to head home, Pat. The celebration is off."

"Are you sure?" said Patrick with a frown.

"Yeah," said SpongeBob as he rose from his bar stool, and he turned to go.

Just then the waiter returned with a towering

ice-cream sundae. "Here's your Triple Gooberberry Sunrise, sir," he told Patrick.

"Yum," said Patrick as he rubbed his starfish tummy and licked his lips.

The wonderful scent of sundae reeled SpongeBob back in.

"Wow! A Triple Gooberberry Sunrise, huh?" said SpongeBob, sitting back down on his stool. "I guess I could use one of those."

"Well, now you're talking!" said Patrick, slapping him on the back. "Hey, waiter! We need another one over here."

"Right away, sir," the waiter replied.

And so began a night of ice cream eating that SpongeBob and Patrick would never forget!

CHAPTER 5

"There you go," said the waiter as he placed a giant sundae in front of SpongeBob.

"Woo!" said SpongeBob.

"Woo-hooo!" said Patrick.

Then they began to eat. Soon spoons were flying and ice cream splattered everywhere—including all over the waiter. And when they were finally done, SpongeBob and Patrick sat back in the chairs and let out two humongous burps!

"Boy, Pat, that hit the spot! I'm feeling better already," said SpongeBob as he rubbed his tummy.

"Yeah," said Patrick.

"Waiter," called SpongeBob. "Let's have another round over here."

Two more Triple Gooberberry Sunrises appeared. In a flash the friends gobbled them up.

"Oh, Mr. Waiter," SpongeBob called, a little jazzed from the sugar. "Two more, please."

The ice cream kept on coming and SpongeBob and Patrick just kept on eating! Soon the sugar was driving them both crazy, and the two friends were getting rowdier by the minute.

"Waaaiter!" SpongeBob cried, splattering ice cream everywhere.

"Oh, waiter," called Patrick.

"Wai-ter! Wai-ter! Wai-ter!" SpongeBob chanted.

The waiter came over and rolled his eyes. "Why do I always get the nuts?"

Totally crazed from a sugar high, SpongeBob and Patrick went goofy. SpongeBob leaped onto the stage and grabbed the microphone.

Draping an arm over the big mechanical peanut, he shouted out, "All right, folks, this one goes out to my two bestest friends in the whole world, Patrick . . . and this peanut guy.

"I love this peanut guy," said the sugared-up

SquarePants. "And in his honor, I'm gonna sing a little ditty we call. . . . 'Waiiii-terrrrrrrrr!'"

SpongeBob and Patrick began to sing loudly and out of tune, chasing the customers away. But they still kept on eating ice cream until they turned purple.

The next morning SpongeBob woke up at the bar. Someone was shaking him—and making the Party Boat spin.

"Hey, come on, buddy," said the waiter. "I want to go home."

SpongeBob opened his eyes. The light hurt.

Slowly, he sat up and blinked. Where am I? he wondered.

SpongeBob looked around. Goofy Goober's was deserted, except for a guy sweeping peanut shells off the floor.

"Come on, pal," said the waiter, helping SpongeBob to his feet.

"Uhhh, my head," groaned SpongeBob. He started to pass out again, but the waiter caught him.

"Look, I'm trying to get out of here," the waiter complained.

"I'll take a Double Fudge Spinny—"

But the waiter cut SpongeBob off. "Listen to me," he said. "It's eight o'clock in the morning. Go scrape up your friend and get going."

"My . . . uh . . . friend?" mumbled SpongeBob.

The waiter pointed at Patrick, who was lying on the floor snoring. His starfish arms and legs were spread out and he was covered from head to toe with ice-cream stains.

"Patrick," SpongeBob cried. "Hey, what's up, buddy?"

Then SpongeBob fell on his face.

The waiter rolled his eyes.

Suddenly SpongeBob jumped to his feet again.

"Wait! You said it was eight o'clock," he cried. "I'm late for work!"

SpongeBob began to panic. "Mr. Krabs is going to be . . ."

Slowly an angry look spread across SpongeBob's face. "Yeah," he hissed. "Mr. Krabs . . ."

With that, SpongeBob bolted for the door.

"Hey, what about your friend?" the waiter cried.

But SpongeBob SquarePants was already gone.

Over at the Krusty Krab 2, Mr. Krabs was looking for new customers with the help of a periscope. It was the start of a busy new day for the finest restaurant in Bikini Bottom.

"Now pay attention, Squidward," said Mr. Krabs. He was teaching Squidward all the tricks of being a manager.

"As the manager you have to keep a sharp eye out for paying customers." As he spoke Mr. Krabs peered through the periscope. Suddenly something caught his attention.

"What's this?" he said.

King Neptune was riding a carriage pulled by a pack of sea horses. Next to the king sat Princess Mindy.

"King Neptune is riding right toward the Krusty Krab!" Mr. Krabs whooped with delight. "Maybe he wants to stop for lunch!"

"Uh-huh," mumbled Squidward, unimpressed.

At this point Mr. Krabs's eyes lit up. "He's got *money!*"

Before the king entered the dining room, Mr. Krabs ran around the restaurant, changing the prices on the menu board.

"A hundred and one dollars for a Krabby Patty!" Squidward cried.

"With cheese, Mr. Tentacles," said Krabs. "With cheese."

Outside, King Neptune stepped down from his carriage and spoke to Mindy.

"Stay in the coach, daughter," he said. "This won't take long."

"Daddy, please, I think you're overreacting."

"Silence, Mindy," the king commanded. "I know what I'm doing."

The king turned—and walked straight into a telephone pole.

"Squire!" yelled the king angrily.

"Yes, Your Highness?" asked the squire.

"Have this pole executed at once!"

Inside the Krusty Krab 2 the squire entered and announced Neptune's arrival with a horn fanfare.

"Prepare thy common selves for King Neptune," the squire declared.

King Neptune entered, and they all bowed their heads.

"There he is, Squidward," said Mr. Krabs, awe-struck. "The richest undersea monarch the world has ever known."

"Then why is he wearing a paper bag on his head?" Squidward asked.

"Greetings, subjects," King Neptune said in a kingly voice. "I seek—"

Suddenly Neptune was interrupted by the squire's second fanfare. He blew and blew until the king finally stuck his finger into the horn, silencing it.

"Oh, sorry," said the squire.

"Ahem," said the king. "Greetings, subjects. I seek the one known as Eugene Krabs. May he present himself to me at once!"

Mr. Krabs stepped forward. "I'm Eugene Krabs, Your Highness. Would you like to order something?"

"Nay!" roared King Neptune angrily. "I am on to you, Krabs! You have stolen the royal crown."

Thunder and lightning followed his each and every word. The king pointed his trident at Mr. Krabs. "You cannot deny what you have done," declared the king. "For as clever as you are, you left a damning piece of evidence at the scene of the crime!"

King Neptune held out the scroll. On it were written these words:

I STOLE YOUR CROWN.
SIGNED,
EUGENE KRABS

Krabs blinked in astonishment as he read the words. The king hurled the scroll to the floor.

"Relinquish the royal crown to me, or I shall be forced to do some very nasty things to you with my *trident*!"

"Bu-but this is crazy! I didn't do it," stammered Mr. Krabs.

Just then the phone rang and the answering machine picked up.

"Ahoy, this is Eugene Krabs. Please leave a message," said the voice on the answering machine.

After the beep a gruff voice spoke.

"Hi, Mr. Krabs. This is Clay, the guy you sold Neptune's crown to. I just wanted to say thanks again for selling me the crown. You know . . . *Neptune's* crown."

Mr. Krabs frantically tried to shut off the answering machine, but it just kept going!

"I sold the crown to a guy in Shell City," said the gruff voice. "And I just wanted to say thanks again for selling me the crown. That's *Neptune's* crown . . . which is now in *Shell City.* Good-bye."

Mr. Krabs ripped the phone off the wall. But it was too late. King Neptune had heard every word.

"Heh, heh, heh," Mr. Krabs laughed nervously. "Don't you just hate wrong numbers?"

King Neptune was not amused.

"You sold my crown to the forbidden Shell City? Whaaaaaaa!" Neptune's scream shook the walls of Mr. Krabs's new restaurant.

At that exact moment, inside a phone booth on the other side of Bikini Bottom, Plankton listened with glee to the results of his incriminating phone call.

"Plan Z . . . I love Plan Z!" he cackled as he hung up the phone.

"Whaaaaaaa!" screamed the king back at the Krusty Krab 2.

He lowered his flame-throwing trident. "Prepare to burn, Krabs!"

"Wait, King Neptune. . . . Please," Krabs whined as the great merman took aim. "I'm beggin' ya! I ain't no crook. Ask anyone. They'll vouch for me."

"Very well then," said King Neptune, lifting his trident. "Before I turn this conniving crustacean into fish meal, who here has anything to say about Eugene Krabs?"

A loud belch turned everyone's eyes to the front door. There stood SpongeBob. He was still a little crazed from the night before. And he was very angry about not getting the promotion.

"I've got something to say about Mr. Krabs," SpongeBob announced.

"SpongeBob, me boy," said Mr. Krabs. "You've come just in time. Please tell King Neptune all about me."

SpongeBob faced the king.

"I've worked for Mr. Krabs for many years and always thought he was the greatest boss," said SpongeBob.

"You see!" cried Mr. Krabs. "A great boss."

"Until today!" SpongeBob continued. "I now realize he's not a great boss. In fact, Mr. Krabs is nothing but a great, big jerk . . . and . . . and . . . he's fat!"

As Mr. Krabs shrank under every word, SpongeBob really let him have it.

"I deserved that manager job, but you didn't give it to me 'cause you say I'm a kid!" yelled SpongeBob. "Well, I'm all man, Krabs, and I've got something to say to you."

SpongeBob stuck out his tongue and gave Mr. Krabs a long, nasty, wet raspberry!

"There," said SpongeBob calmly. "I think I've made my point."

King Neptune looked around.

"Anyone else?" he roared.

"Nobody else? Well then . . ."

With that, King Neptune lowered his crackling trident once more—and aimed it right at Mr. Krabs!

CHAPTER 6

Mr. Krabs was shaking in his shell. Then a bolt of lightning burst from King Neptune's staff and hit him in the backside! Mr. Krabs howled and hopped around the restaurant, smoke pouring from his pants.

"Me pants are on fire," screamed Mr. Krabs. "Me underwear's on fire. I'M ON FIRE!"

Mr. Krabs dived into a tub of water and put out the fire. As his bottom sizzled, he sighed with relief.

King Neptune laughed. Then he aimed his trident once again.

"And now, Eugene Krabs . . . you will be punished!" he declared.

But before the king could unleash another lightning

bolt, SpongeBob SquarePants jumped in front of his boss and cried, "Wait!"

"Wha—?" said Neptune.

"I'm flattered you would do this on my account," said SpongeBob. "But being manager isn't worth punishing Mr. Krabs over."

Neptune's eyes grew stormy.

"Quiet, fool!" he hollered. "Mr. Krabs stole my crown and sold it to Shell City. That's why he must be punished."

SpongeBob scratched his square head.

"Gee, doesn't it seem a little harsh to punish someone over a crown?" he asked.

Neptune shook his head. "You don't understand. My crown is a symbol of my kinglike authority"—the King leaned over and whispered—"and just between you and me, my hair is thinning a bit."

"Ah, Your Highness. I'm sure it's not that noticeable," said SpongeBob.

The king considered SpongeBob's words. Then, standing tall, Neptune pulled the paper bag off of his head. The glare on his bald spot was so strong, it practically blinded everyone.

"Aaaaaaaaaagghhh! Bald! Bald!" screeched SpongeBob, pointing at the chrome dome and shielding his eyes.

Reddening, Neptune quickly placed the bag back on his head.

"All right, all right, that's enough," he said.

SpongeBob now understood how important the crown was to the king. He tugged at Neptune's beard.

"King Neptune, sir," said SpongeBob, "would you spare Mr. Krabs from punishment if I went and got your crown back?"

"You!" bellowed Neptune. "Go to Shell City?"

The king laughed out loud.

"The road to Shell City is the most dangerous journey that any man can undertake," said the king. "What chance would you have? You're just a kid."

"But I'm not a kid. I can do it," said SpongeBob.

Neptune simply shook his head and tapped SpongeBob's behind with his long trident.

"Run along," he told the square little sponge.

"I have a crab to cook," said the king.

Then, once more, Neptune aimed his trident at Mr. Krabs.

"Aaaahhh!" screamed Krabs.

"NO! I won't let you," said SpongeBob, standing in front of his boss again.

"Very well then," King Neptune replied. "I'll have to punish you both!"

SpongeBob hugged Mr. Krabs. Mr. Krabs hugged SpongeBob back. They both knew they were in big trouble, and they screamed together.

"AAAAHHHHHHHHH!"

Just then Princess Mindy appeared, blocking her father's aim.

"Daddy, stop it!" she cried. "Can't you get through one day without punishing someone?"

"Mindy," said Neptune sternly. "I told you to stay in the carriage."

"Where's your love and compassion?" said Mindy. She took SpongeBob by the arm. "Look at this little guy. He's willing to risk his life to find your crown and save his boss."

"But, daughter—," said Neptune.

"Please, Father," said Mindy. "At least let him try. What have you got to lose? Might I remind you of your special problem?"

Mindy reached up and pulled the bag off her father's head.

"Bald! Bald! Bald! Ahhhh! My eyes!" screamed a crowd of customers.

King Neptune sighed a mighty sigh and then surrendered.

"Very well, Mindy," said the king. "I'll give him a chance. But when your little champion fails to return, I get to cook this crab but good!"

Mr. Krabs began to shake again.

"And as for you," Neptune said to SpongeBob, "be back here with my crown in exactly ten days."

Suddenly Patrick the starfish entered the restaurant and spoke up. "He can do it in nine!"

"Eight!" called the king.

"Seven," boasted Patrick.

"Six!" roared the king.

"Fi—"

Before Patrick could say another word, Mr. Krabs and SpongeBob shouted "Patrick!" and they tackled him.

On the ground Mr. Krabs placed his claw over Patrick's big mouth before he made things worse.

"Six it is, then," commanded the king.

"Five!" said Patrick. But SpongeBob shushed him.

The king lifted his trident once again. "Until then the crab shall remain frozen where he now stands."

Mr. Krabs threw up his hands. "No! Wait! I'm begging you—"

But it was too late. An icy ray blasted out of Neptune's trident, cooling the Krusty Krab 2's dining room.

"Humph," said Squidward. "Who turned on the air conditioner?"

Then he spied Mr. Krabs. His boss was now encased in a block of ice.

"Ahhh! Mr. Krabs," screamed Squidward.

He hurried to Mr. Krabs's side and pounded on the ice that imprisoned him.

"Oh, no, this is terrible," cried Squidward, holding his head in his tentacles. "Who's gonna sign my paycheck?"

"Come along, Mindy," commanded King Neptune. Then the mighty monarch of the sea turned on his heels and stormed out the front door.

Mindy hurried over to speak with SpongeBob and Patrick.

"Listen, you guys. The road to Shell City is really dangerous. There are crooks, bullies, and monsters everywhere," she warned.

SpongeBob's eyes went wide. Patrick just stared at Mindy, awestruck. He had never seen a mermaid before—let alone one so beautiful!

"And what's worse," added Mindy, "there's a giant Cyclops who guards the outskirts of the city and preys on innocent sea creatures."

Now SpongeBob was shaking.

"Don't let him catch you, because if he does he'll take you back to his lair and you'll never be seen again!"

"She's purdy, SpongeBob," Patrick whispered. He

was completely smitten by Mindy's beauty.

"Here, take this," said Mindy. She handed SpongeBob a sack that was tied at the top.

"What's in here?" SpongeBob asked. Before Mindy could reply, he peeked inside the bag. A huge wind blew out, nearly tearing SpongeBob's face off!

"It's a magical bag of winds," Mindy explained. "I stole it from my father."

"You're hot!" Patrick told the mermaid.

Mindy ignored him.

"Once you find the crown, open the bag of winds and you'll be blown back home."

"Gee, thanks!" said SpongeBob.

"Mindy!" King Neptune yelled from the carriage. "Come along. Time to go back to the castle."

"I'm coming!" she called. Then she faced the boys. "Good luck, SpongeBob."

Mindy turned to go.

"Wait!" SpongeBob cried. "How did you know my name?"

Mindy shrugged. "Oh, I'm going to be queen of

the sea one day. I've learned the names of all the sea creatures."

"What's my name?" Patrick asked shyly.

"That's easy," Mindy replied. "You're Patrick Star."

"Heh . . . aheee . . . aheh," said Patrick. Then he fainted.

"MINDY!" the king roared.

"I've got to go," said Mindy. Then she smiled at them. "I believe in you guys."

"Thanks, Mindy," called SpongeBob as the mermaid princess swam away.

Now that the king and his daughter were gone, SpongeBob walked up to his frozen boss to console him.

"Don't worry, Mr. Krabs. Patrick, Squidward, and I—"

"Pass!" said Squidward.

"Er, ah . . . Patrick and I—"

"Hi!" Patrick waved.

"We are gonna save you from Neptune's wrath. You've got nothing to worry about. Your life is in our hands."

Mr. Krabs's frozen face looked down at them. Even through the thick layers of magical ice, they could hear the restaurant owner groan.

But SpongeBob SquarePants wasn't discouraged. In fact, he was filled with determination. There was a steely glint in his spongy eyes as he grabbed Patrick's arm and said, "Let's go get that crown!"

CHAPTER 7

"Let's go, Patrick!" yelled SpongeBob.

Together they hurried to the back of Krusty Krab 2. SpongeBob unlocked a secret door behind the deep fryer. The door swung open and they leaped onto the poles.

A minute later both were down in Mr. Krabs's secret basement.

"It's dark and scary down here," said Patrick fearfully.

"Here we are," SpongeBob announced.

"I didn't know this was down here!" cried Patrick.

"Krabs has a lot of secrets," SpongeBob whispered.

Then SpongeBob led his friend through a hidden door and into a dark room.

"Feast your eyes, Patrick," announced SpongeBob, and he flipped on the lights.

Patrick's eyes popped out. "What is it?"

"The Patty Wagon," SpongeBob replied, stepping around a vehicle built to look like a Krabby Patty.

"Mr. Krabs uses it for promotional reasons," SpongeBob explained. "Let me show you some of its features. . . ."

As they stepped around the giant burger SpongeBob pointed out the details.

"Sesame seed finish . . . steel-belted pickles . . . grilled leather interior . . . and under the hood a fuel-injected french fryer with dual overhead greasetraps!"

"Wow," Patrick exclaimed.

"Yeah, wow," SpongeBob agreed, and then he hopped behind the wheel.

"Hey," said Patrick. "I thought you didn't have a driver's license."

SpongeBob rolled his eyes. "You don't need a license to drive a *sandwich,* Patrick."

"Oh."

Patrick climbed aboard. They fastened their safety belts. Then SpongeBob turned the ignition key.

The fryer under the hood began to boil. The smell of french fries shot out the exhaust pipe. Then they roared up the exit ramp.

A garage door opened. Sesame seeds were flying everywhere as the Patty Wagon flew out the back of the Krusty Krab 2.

"Shell City, here we come!" yelled SpongeBob and Patrick in unison. Then SpongeBob pressed the Patty Wagon's fuel pedal to the grilled leather floor.

In a cloud, the Patty Wagon hurtled down the roadway at top speed.

SpongeBob grinned. Now they were *really* cooking!

Inside the Krusty Krab 2 poor Mr. Krabs was still frozen solid.

Above the restaurant's front door, the bells chimed.

"Ding-a-ling," said Plankton, marching in with an evil grin.

The Chum Bucket's owner walked right up to Mr. Krabs. "Hey, there, old buddy—freeze!" he cried.

Chuckling at his own bad joke, Plankton sat down at a table across from Mr. Krabs.

"I'd like one secret formula to go," he told his rival.

When Mr. Krabs didn't move, Plankton laughed.

"No, no," he said. "Don't trouble yourself, Krabs. I'll get it."

Plankton ran into the kitchen and tore the place apart. A few minutes later he came out holding a little bottle. Its label read SECRET FORMULA.

Then Plankton walked right toward the Krabcube and approached the front door.

"Well," said Plankton, "I'd like to hang around, but I've got Krabby Patties to make over at the Chum Bucket." He laughed maniacally. "Plan Z, I love ya!"

Still laughing, Plankton walked out.

Inside his block of ice, a single tear rolled down Mr. Krabs's cheek.

The engine sizzled like a Krabby Patty frying on the grill as the Patty Wagon rolled up one side of a hill and down another. The headlights lit up a sign directly in front of them that read COUNTY LINE.

"Hey, we're almost there," said SpongeBob.

While they drove, the boys sang the Goofy Goober song, over and over again.

"I'm a Goofy Goober, yeah! You're a Goofy Goober, yeah! We're all Goofy Goobers, yeah!"

SpongeBob spied a gas station and pulled up to the pump. Two gas station attendants came out and gawked at the Patty Wagon. One of them wore overalls with FLOYD on the pocket. The other fellow's name tag read LLOYD.

"Fill 'er up, please," said SpongeBob.

"What'll it be, fellas, mustard or ketchup?" asked Floyd. Then the two attendants laughed and slapped their knees.

"Are they laughing at us?" Patrick asked.

SpongeBob raised his hand. "Don't worry, Patrick. I know how to handle the rural folk."

SpongeBob stepped out of the car and faced the two gas station attendants.

"I assure you gentlemen that this vehicle runs on high octane unleaded," SpongeBob informed them coolly. "The *mustard* goes in the windshield washer."

The gas station guys watched as SpongeBob demonstrated. He carefully lifted the mustard nozzle and filled up the windshield washer container. When it was full, he closed the container and hung the nozzle back in its place. But the guys at the gas station just laughed even harder.

"You see that, Lloyd," cackled Floyd. "The *mustard* goes in the windshield washer!"

SpongeBob was not amused.

"Where're you dumb kids heading, anyway?" added Floyd.

"*Kids?*" said Patrick angrily.

"Now, Patrick," said SpongeBob, holding his friend back.

"For your information, we are not kids," SpongeBob said in a matter-of-fact tone. "We

It's the grand opening of the Krusty Krab 2, and SpongeBob is sure he will be chosen to be the new manager . . .

m ready! Promotion!"

"I'm ready! Depression!"

but Mr. Krabs gives the job to Squidward.

With Patrick's help, SpongeBob decides to drown his sorrows in ice-cream sundaes!

Meanwhile Plankton comes up with a plan to steal the Krabby Patty formula. . . .

SpongeBob and Patrick offer to
help save Mr. Krabs.

"I'm on to you,
Krabs! You've
stolen the royal
crown."

So King Neptune holds
Mr. Krabs prisoner—and freezes
him—until SpongeBob and Patrick
return with the crown.

SpongeBob and Patrick
set off on an adventure
to find King Neptune's crown
and save Mr. Krabs.

"We'll never be able to save Mr. Krabs. We're just kids!"

Mindy turns SpongeBob and Patrick into men . . .

by giving them mustaches.

SpongeBob and Patrick
retrieve the crown . . .

"I've got the secret recipe!"

and head
home—with a
little help
from a friend.

Meanwhile Plankton's plan is in full effect—he has taken over Bikini Bottom.

"All hail Plankton!"

are *men* and we are on our way to Shell City."

"Shell City?" said Floyd. "Ain't that the place guarded by a killer Cyclops?"

"That's right," SpongeBob replied.

Floyd and Lloyd suddenly stopped laughing and a serious look spread across their faces.

"Lloyd, take off your hat in respect," said Floyd grimly. "Respect for the doomed!"

Then they both laughed again.

"You two dipsticks ain't gonna last ten seconds over the county line," said Lloyd.

"Oh, yeah?" said SpongeBob. "We'll just see about that!"

He and Patrick hopped back into the car and gunned the engine. Then they drove across the county line.

Moments later an armed thug with a crowbar came at them.

"Out of the car, fellas," said the thug.

The boys climbed out of the Patty Wagon and the thug hopped in. He gunned the engine and drove away in a cloud of bubbles.

"How many seconds was that?" asked SpongeBob.

The gas station attendants checked their watches. "Twelve," said Lloyd.

"In your face!" cried SpongeBob.

Patrick and SpongeBob started to laugh.

"That's what I'm talking about," said SpongeBob, gloating. "Twelve is *two whole seconds* more than ten!"

"Yeah!" said Patrick. "Who's the kid now?"

Laughing, SpongeBob and Patrick walked away. As they disappeared around the corner, Lloyd looked at his friend.

"Yup," he said. "They're doomed."

CHAPTER 8

The Chum Bucket was suddenly the most popular restaurant in Bikini Bottom! Customers lined up around the block to get into the hot new eatery. Plankton had done a brilliant job of redecorating. The walls had been freshly painted. The floors had been redone and the furniture was brand-new. But the big draw was the delicious food.

"That's right," shouted Plankton through a bullhorn. "The Chum Bucket has got Krabby Patties. Get them while they're hot and delicious."

Just then reporter Perch Perkins sauntered into the Chum Bucket. He walked right up to Plankton.

"Excuse me, Plankton," he said. "I'm Perch

Perkins, Action News. Can I get a minute of your time?"

"Anything for you, Perch," Plankton answered with a phony smile on his face.

"All of Bikini Bottom wants to know. *How* did you get the Krabby Patty?" asked Perch Perkins, shoving his microphone under Plankton's nose.

"Well, Perch, before my dear friend Eugene Krabs was frozen by King Neptune," said Plankton, pausing to wipe away a phony tear, "Krabs confided in me a secret wish—in the event that his criminal past ever caught up with him."

Plankton sighed theatrically. "He said, 'Sell the Krabby Patty in my absence at the Chum Bucket. Don't let the flame die out.'"

"Wow," said Perch Perkins, touched.

"And there's a Chum Bucket helmet free with every purchase!" added Plankton brightly, and handed Perch a bucket-shaped helmet with the words "Chum Bucket" written on it.

"Thanks," said the newsman.

Plankton started throwing bucket helmets to

everyone in the Chum Bucket. "Bucket helmets for everyone!" he cried. "Here you go, sir!"

"Thanks!" said a fish.

Plankton gave a bucket helmet to Mrs. Puff. "Here's yours, ma'am."

"Why, thank you," said Mrs. Puff.

"Helmets for the whole family," said Plankton as he circled a big table. He placed a bucket helmet on everyone sitting there.

"Thanks!" said the newly bucket-helmet-headed family.

With a wave to all of his new customers, Plankton ran into the kitchen.

"Karen, baby," he told his computer wife. "I haven't felt this giddy since the day you agreed to be my wife."

"I never agreed," replied Karen the Computer.

Plankton ignored her.

"Evil Plan Z is working perfectly," he said instead. "Nothing can stop me now."

"I hate to be the one to tell you this," said Karen. "But my sensors have indicated that SpongeBob and his pink friend are going after the crown. If they make it back, Neptune might see some fingerprints."

Karen stared at Plankton's little hands.

"Tiny fingerprints," she added. "Stubby, tiny fingerprints."

Plankton stared down at his hands and frowned. Then he put them into his pockets.

"Evil Plan Z is way ahead of you," he said. "I've already hired someone to take care of those two. His name is Dennis. He's a really big scary dude who rides a huge motorcycle."

Back at the gas station near the county line, a huge motorcycle pulled up to the pump. Behind the handlebars sat Dennis, a really big scary dude.

Cutting the engine to a rumble, Dennis spied a spot on the concrete. He lowered the brim on his cowboy hat and crouched down. Then he sniffed the concrete.

"Mustard," he murmured.

"Hey, mister," hooted Lloyd, the gas station attendant. "Does that hat take ten gallons?"

The gas station guys laughed and laughed—until the big scary dude knocked each of them over. Flat on their backs, Floyd and Lloyd were in no position to be laughing.

Not so very far down the road, SpongeBob and Patrick trudged along. They tried to sing to keep up their spirits, but they were just too tired.

"All right . . . huff . . . oh, yeah . . . puff . . . ," wheezed SpongeBob.

"Are we there yet?" Patrick whined.

"We must be close now," said SpongeBob. Then he spotted a sign.

"Hey, Patrick! Look. Shell City, straight ahead."

They read the sign, which was partly hidden by some seaweed. It read SHELL CITY, ONLY FIVE DAYS.

"Wow!" said SpongeBob. "Only five days away—"

Then the wind blew the seaweed away—and the rest of the sign was uncovered.

"—BY CAR!?!" cried SpongeBob.

Patrick slapped his head and SpongeBob's shoulders sagged.

"At this rate we're never going to make it back in

six days," said SpongeBob. "If only we still had our car."

Patrick grabbed his square friend's arm. "SpongeBob, look—it's our car!"

It was the Patty Wagon, parked next to a sunken tugboat. Music and voices seemed to be coming from inside the tugboat, called the Thug Tug.

"Let's hurry, Pat," SpongeBob cried, "before the thug who stole our car comes back."

But when they reached their car, something important was missing.

"The key!" SpongeBob cried.

"Where do you think it is?" Patrick asked.

SpongeBob faced the tugboat just as a terrified fish was tossed through the window.

"This looks like a nice place," said Patrick.

But SpongeBob wasn't so sure.

Cautiously the two friends crept up to the window and peered inside. Tough-looking thugs were shooting pool, throwing back drinks, and acting tough.

Suddenly SpongeBob spotted the thug who stole the Patty Wagon. He was shooting pool with some other fish. Hanging from his belt, SpongeBob spotted a gleaming object.

"There it is, Pat. The key!" cried SpongeBob. Then he frowned. "But how are we going to get it?"

"I know," said Patrick. "Walk in and ask for it."

SpongeBob shook his head. "Patrick. That's a terrible idea."

"Sorry."

"I know!" said SpongeBob, snapping his fingers. "I'll go in and create a distraction. Then you grab the key."

"Ooo, ooo, wait!" Patrick cried, hopping from tentacle to tentacle. "I want to do the distraction."

SpongeBob shrugged. "Okay. I guess it doesn't really matter who does the distraction."

Remembering an old Western movie he'd seen, Patrick swaggered right up to the front door and threw it open. Then he boldly stepped inside. SpongeBob crept in behind his pink friend, trying not to be seen.

"Can I have everybody's attention!" yelled Patrick.

The music stopped and all heads turned toward

the front door. Dozens of mean-looking eyes stared at the young starfish, waiting for him to speak again.

"I have to use the bathroom," announced Patrick.

One of the thugs pointed to a door next to the phone booth. "It's right over there."

The thug at the pool table looked down. There was SpongeBob, tugging on the Patty Wagon key hanging from his belt.

"Oh, *there* it is," SpongeBob said, rubbing his eye. "Stupid contact lenses."

SpongeBob pretended to pick something off the ground.

"I'd better go wash it off," he said, and bolted for the restroom.

"Patrick!" he cried, pushing through the door. "You call that a distraction?"

"I had to go to the bathroom," Patrick replied sheepishly.

SpongeBob looked down at his hands. They were filthy from fumbling on the floor.

"I got my hands dirty for nothing," he said, disgusted.

SpongeBob pumped the soap dispenser. Bubbles popped out and floated around the bathroom.

"Patrick! Check it out!"

"Whoa!" cried Patrick.

"Hooray! Bubble party!" SpongeBob said, and they began to squirt more bubbles. The two giggled and danced and lathered up as bubbles filled the bathroom.

Some of the bubbles started to leak out of the restroom door. Suddenly the music in the next room stopped and someone yelled in an angry voice.

"Hey! Who blew this bubble?" yelled Victor, the bartender.

"Not me, Victor," said a frightened thug.

"I didn't," cried another. "I hate soap."

"You all know the rules," Victor yelled.

The tug thugs all nodded.

"Any and all bubble-blowing babies gets kicked out of the bar," said one of the thugs.

"That's right," roared Victor. "So who blew it?"

Inside the bathroom SpongeBob and Patrick could hear all the yelling going on in the bar, and they were frantically trying to pop all the bubbles before they were caught.

"So nobody knows, eh?" said Victor, looking around. "Well, I know. I know that somebody in here is a bubble blower."

SpongeBob and Patrick left the bubbleless bathroom and tried to sneak out the back door.

"You!" said Victor, pointing at them. "We're on a bubble-blower hunt. And don't think we don't know how to weed them out."

Victor had everyone in the tugboat line up so he could inspect them. When everyone was in a neat row, he turned to his disc jockey.

"DJ, time for the test," he called.

The DJ fumbled behind the speaker and put on the Goofy Goober theme song.

"No bubble blower can resist singing along to this," Victor snarled.

"SpongeBob," Patrick whined. "It's the Goofy Goober theme song!"

"I know," said SpongeBob.

The music began to play—loudly—and SpongeBob

and Patrick struggled desperately against the urge to sing along.

One of the tough guys coughed and Victor rushed up to him.

"It was you!" he cried. "*You're* the bubble-blowing baby!"

"No, no," the thug said. "I only coughed. I swear."

Sneering, Victor moved down the line. Nobody had cracked yet, so Victor called to the disc jockey, "Turn it up louder!"

The music swelled, filling the tug with the perfect sing-along tune. Sweat was pouring down SpongeBob's head. His foot began to tap, but he managed to step on it with his other foot.

Patrick appeared ready to break.

"*Don't* sing along, Patrick," SpongeBob whispered.

"I'm trying," Patrick said. "I'm trying *so* hard!"

SpongeBob looked up to see Victor towering over him.

"Don't you know the words?" Victor growled. "I'm a Goofy Goober, yeah! You're a Goofy Goober . . ."

SpongeBob and Patrick resisted singing along with the tune for as long as they could.

Finally someone cracked.

"I'm a Goofy Goober, yeah! Goofy, Goofy, Goober, Goober—"

"Well, well, well," said Victor.

SpongeBob and Patrick breathed sighs of relief as Victor rushed up to two Siamese twin fish.

"Which one of you babies was it?" he roared.

The two fish pointed to each other. "It was him!" they cried.

"Well," said Victor with a nasty grin. "Looks like we've got ourselves a double bubble-blowing baby."

The Siamese fish tried to swim away, but the thugs chased them.

With everyone running around, SpongeBob and Patrick managed to escape.

"Man, that was a close call," sighed SpongeBob once they were outside the tugboat of thugs.

"Guess what I got," said Patrick with a goofy smile.

He pulled the Patty Wagon's key out of his pocket.

"The key!" SpongeBob cried. "Oh, Pat, I could kiss you."

They ran to the Patty Wagon and started the engine. The Goofy Goober theme song blasted out of the speaker.

SpongeBob turned off the sound system, pulled out the CD, and smashed it. It landed on the ground right next to two bottles of bubbles. Then the Patty Wagon sped off into the night.

CHAPTER 9

Back in Bikini Bottom, Plankton's plot was kicking into high gear, as a certain grumpy squid was about to find out.

"One more lap around town and it's a frosty beverage for you, Squiddy!" Squidward promised himself as he pedaled his bicycle.

He was daydreaming about that refreshing treat when he saw something odd: a fish with a chum bucket on its head. Not a *real* chum bucket, but a bucket-shaped helmet.

"Morning," said the bucket-headed fish.

"Some people have no taste in headgear," Squidward muttered to himself.

Then he saw another fish with a bucket on her head.

"Egads! Must be contagious," Squidward declared.

Soon he was seeing chum buckets everywhere! Squidward even saw a mother fish pushing a baby carriage full of baby fish wearing buckets on their heads!

Squidward was horrified. "Babies, too? Now that's just hideous for several reasons."

At the traffic light he stopped next to a woman's car. She was also wearing a Chum Bucket helmet.

"Excuse me, Mrs. Puff, but where is everyone getting that horrid headwear?"

"I got it at the Chum Bucket," Mrs. Puff replied. "Plankton's giving them away free with every Krabby Patty."

"Chum Bucket?" cried Squidward. "Free? Krabby Patty? Plankton? Giving? With?"

"That's right," called Mrs. Puff as she zoomed away.

Squidward scratched his bald squid head. "Something smells fishy around here, and for once it isn't my laundry."

Squidward pedaled right over to the Chum

Bucket. The place was hopping. Squidward burst through the door.

"All right, Plankton. I want a word with you."

"Hello, Squidward," Plankton said, grinning smugly. "Did you stop by to get your free bucket helmet?"

"No," said Squidward. "You may have hood-winked everyone else in this backwater town, but you can't fool me. I listen to public radio!"

Plankton made an innocent face. "And what is *that* supposed to mean?"

Squidward shook his finger under Plankton's nose.

"It means you set up Mr. Krabs," he cried. "You stole the crown so Neptune would freeze him and you could finally get your stubby little paws on the Krabby Patty formula. It was *you* all along!"

Plankton gave Squidward a wounded look. But the crusty old squid wasn't buying it.

"I haven't solved the whole bucket-helmet give-away part yet, but maybe Neptune and I can get to the bottom of it together," said Squidward, turning to go. "I'm going to go talk to King Neptune right now!" he yelled. Then Squidward slammed the door and was gone.

"Tell him I said hello," Plankton called, "if you make it that far."

Plankton laughed like some kind of stubby-fingered madman.

"Now it's time to start the next phase of Plan Z. The *really* evil part."

He tapped a few keys on Karen the Computer.

"Helmet brain control activated," Karen said.

◆◆◆◆◆◆◆◆

In every home, in every shop, all over Bikini Bottom, a strange thing was happening.

All those trendy Chum Bucket helmet hats sitting atop all those heads began to *change*. With a buzz and a click, they took control of everyone's mind.

"All hail Plankton! All hail Plankton!" chanted the people of Bikini Bottom.

Soon an army of bucket heads filled the streets.

"All hail Plankton! All hail Plankton!"

They poured out of houses and shops. From

under rocks, from the reefs, and from the trenches, all the sea life marched together. And they all chanted together.

"All hail Plankton! All hail Plankton!"

Plankton ran to the window and peered through his telescope. There they were—his army of mind-controlled bucket heads.

Plankton hopped up and down with glee.

"Plan Z! Plan Z!"

Outside, the crowd spoke with one voice.

"All hail Plankton! All hail Plankton!"

CHAPTER 10

Out on the open road, SpongeBob and Patrick were speeding along the highway.

"Come on, Pat. One more time," said SpongeBob.

Patrick stood up and started to imitate the bartender from the Thug Tug.

"We're on a bubble-blower hunt, and don't think we don't know how to weed 'em out."

SpongeBob and Patrick both started hysterically laughing. Meanwhile the scenery around them began to change. They were passing piles of skulls and bones, but neither noticed.

"Weed 'em out!" cried SpongeBob.

"What a jerk!" yelled Patrick.

"How about when he was all like, 'Well, looks like

we've got ourselves a double bubble-blowing baby,'" said SpongeBob.

"And they were like, 'It wasn't us! It wasn't us!'" added Patrick.

They continued to laugh and laugh until the car started to shake violently.

SpongeBob stopped laughing. "The road's getting kind of bumpy here."

They made it over the bumpy bones and were back on a smooth road.

"You know, SpongeBob," said Patrick, "there's a lesson to be learned from all this."

"What's that, Patrick?"

"A double bubble-blowing baby doesn't belong out here . . . in man's country."

"Yeah . . . wait!" cried SpongeBob. "We blew that bubble. Doesn't that make us the double bubble-blowing baby?"

They both stared off in the distance, as if they were contemplating what SpongeBob had just said, when Patrick spotted an ice-cream stand.

"Look!" cried Patrick. "Free ice cream!"

SpongeBob turned off the main road and pulled up next to the ice-cream stand.

"Oh, boy!" exclaimed SpongeBob. He jumped out of the car and into a pile of bones and kept walking toward the ice cream.

Patrick looked around at the pile of bones. "Wait a minute. . . . Wait a minute!" cried Patrick. "SpongeBob!"

"What?"

"Make mine a chocolate!" said Patrick.

SpongeBob approached the old lady in the ice-cream stand.

"Two, please."

"Certainly," she said.

A few minutes later the old woman handed them two big sloppy sundaes.

"You kids enjoy," she told them.

"We're men, lady, but thanks," said SpongeBob. Then he turned to Patrick. "Okay, let's go— hey!"

SpongeBob tried to leave the ice-cream hut, but the old lady wouldn't let go of his ice cream!

SpongeBob began to tug and pull, but he was stuck as if his hands were glued there.

Suddenly the ground began to rumble.

SpongeBob struggled to get away, even as the walls of the ice-cream stand fell. The old lady started to look less and less like an old lady.

"What kind of old lady are you?" cried SpongeBob.

Just then her wig and glasses fell off. And SpongeBob felt himself being lifted off the ground.

"Ewwwwwww!" he screamed.

Snapping fangs and two bulging eyes broke out of the ground—followed by a monstrous Frog Fish. The "old lady" was just part of the monster's tongue! This was a trap!

"AAAAAAAAGGGGGGGGGGGGHHHH!" screamed SpongeBob.

Finally he let go of the ice cream.

SpongeBob bounced off a fang and fell into the Patty Wagon. Luckily, Patrick backed up just in time.

"Did you get the ice cream?" asked Patrick.

"Step on it, Patrick!" SpongeBob yelled.

Steel-belted pickles spun in the dirt, and the Patty Wagon raced away. SpongeBob, clinging to the dashboard (the Wagon was a convertible—no roof), looked over his shoulder.

The Frog Fish was gaining on them! SpongeBob let out a bloodcurdling scream,

"AAAAAAGGGGGGHHHHHH!"

The hungry, fanged mouth was about to swallow the Patty Wagon! The old lady popped out of the monster's mouth.

"Come on, kiddies," she cackled. "Have some ice cream."

Patrick and SpongeBob screamed some more.

"I'll let you pet Mr. Whiskers," the old lady said.

A little phony cat poked out of the Frog Fish's mouth and meowed.

"Jump for it, Patrick!" SpongeBob cried.

They both leaped from the Patty Wagon—just as it flew over the edge of a cliff. The jaws of the Frog Fish snapped shut, swallowing the Patty Wagon. The monster smiled and made a yummy noise.

Suddenly the Frog Fish realized it had leaped out

over the deep trench—with nothing to hold it up.

And then things got even worse for the Frog Fish.

SpongeBob and Patrick watched as a humongous leaping serpent hopped out of the trench and swallowed the Frog Fish whole, like it was a tiny gold fish.

SpongeBob and Patrick just stood there staring into the abyss.

"Well, we lost our car *again*," said SpongeBob.

"Never mind the car," said Patrick. "Where is the road?"

Patrick's voice echoed across the trench. "Road . . . road . . . road . . . road . . ."

"There's the road," said SpongeBob, "on the other side of this deep, dark, dangerous, monster-infested trench."

A nasty roar floated up from below.

"Hey, SpongeBob, look!" said Patrick. "I found the way down."

Patrick began to step onto the stairs that went right down into the trench.

Patrick looked into the darkness. More growls and snarls rose from the pit.

"Well," said Patrick, trying to sound cheerful, "we're not gonna get the crown standing here. On to Shell City, right, SpongeBob?"

But SpongeBob had turned around. With his shoulders slumped, and a frown on his face, he was walking away.

"SpongeBob?" cried Patrick. "Hey, where are you going?"

"I'm going home, Patrick."

Patrick was surprised. "But what about Mr. Krabs?"

"What about us?" said SpongeBob. "We'll never survive in that trench. We're just . . . *kids*."

"We're not kids," insisted Patrick.

"Open your eyes, Patrick!" SpongeBob cried. "We blow bubbles. We eat ice cream! We worship a dancing peanut, for cripe's sake! We don't belong out here!"

"We do not worship him," said Patrick.

SpongeBob pulled down Patrick's shorts. The

starfish was wearing Goofy Goober undies.

"Patrick," SpongeBob said sternly, "you have been wearing the same Goofy Goober Peanut Party underpants for three years straight. What do you call that?"

"Worship!" Patrick sobbed, shorts still down around his ankles. "You're right, SpongeBob. We *are* kids."

Patrick tried to run home, but he tripped over his shorts.

"Pull your pants up, Patrick," SpongeBob told him. "We're going home."

"But you can't go home," said a familiar voice.

Patrick looked up and saw—

"Mindy!"

He struggled to pull up his pants, but it didn't work. They just fell down again.

"How much did you hear?" asked SpongeBob.

"I head enough," replied Mindy.

"Did you see my underwear?" Patrick asked as he prepared to pull up his pants again.

"Look, you guys. You may be kids, but you're the

only ones left who can get that crown," said Mindy.

"What are you talking about?" asked SpongeBob.

"Things have gotten a lot worse since you left Bikini Bottom," Mindy said as she opened a clam-shaped mirror that doubled as a spy camera. "Or should I say . . . Planktopolis!"

She showed them in her mirror what had become of their hometown. Plankton laughed diabolically as he forced a whole bucket-headed army of mind-numbed slaves to build a huge monument in his honor.

"Work harder! Work harder!" Plankton cried, snapping a whip.

SpongeBob watched this scene in horror.

"Oh, my gosh, it's true!" cried SpongeBob. "Everyone I know is a slave!

"Mrs. Puff! Squidward!" he cried.

Then he gasped. "Gary!"

"Meow Plankton," murmured Gary.

"Why doesn't King Neptune stop this?" SpongeBob asked.

Mindy sighed. "My father is too distracted by his bald spot to help anyone."

She closed her compact and faced them. "So you see, you guys have got to get to Shell City. The entire fate of Bikini Bottom rests in your hands."

SpongeBob pleaded, "But . . . but we're just—"

"Hey, it doesn't matter if you're kids. And what's so wrong with being a kid, anyway? Kids rule! You don't need to be a man to do this. You just gotta believe in yourself!" cried Mindy.

"I believe—," cried SpongeBob, throwing his fist in the air.

"That's the spirit!" exclaimed Mindy.

"I believe that Mr. Krabs is a gonerrrrrrrrr!" finished SpongeBob as he burst into tears.

Patrick started crying too. "And don't forget our homeland," he added, sniffling.

"Come on, guys," said Mindy.

But SpongeBob and Patrick were inconsolable. They both collapsed to the ground in hysterics.

❖❖❖❖❖❖❖❖❖

Meanwhile, back at the Thug Tug, a motorcycle pulled up with a roar and a cloud of sand. Sitting in the saddle was Dennis, the really big scary dude.

He scanned the area, looking for clues, and he found one: The remnants of popped bubbles were lying in the parking lot.

"Hmmm," he grunted, "looks like they left this here." He picked up the bottle and blew a bubble.

"Hey," yelled Victor from the Thug Tug's doorway, "you may not know it, cowboy, but we've got a rule around here about blowing bubbles."

Victor snapped his fingers and a dozen thug fish appeared. Every one of them was spoiling for a fight.

The thugs surrounded Dennis, and Victor walked right up to him. "The rule says that all bubble blowers will be punished."

But Dennis picked up Victor and sent him flying all the way back to the Thug Tug.

Dennis tipped his cowboy hat and sped away on his motorcycle, hot on SpongeBob's trail.

◆❖◆❖◆❖◆❖◆❖◆

By this time SpongeBob and Patrick were cradling each other—and *still* crying. Mindy watched them cry, unsure what to do.

"Oh, boy. Hmmm. . . . Think, Mindy, think," she mumbled to herself.

Finally an idea came to mind. "Well, I guess you're right. A couple of kids could never survive this journey," she said.

SpongeBob and Patrick just looked at each other and started crying again.

"That's why I'll just have to turn you into men," said Mindy.

Suddenly smiles spread across their faces, and the boys stopped crying and began jumping up and down.

"You can do that? How?" asked SpongeBob.

"With my mermaid magic," said Mindy.

"Did you hear that, Pat?" SpongeBob said, excited. "She'll use her mermaid magic to turn us into men!"

"Hooray!" cried SpongeBob and Patrick. "We're going to be men! We're going to be men!"

"Now, let's get started," said Mindy. "Close your eyes."

They did.

"Are we men yet?" asked SpongeBob impatiently.

"Not yet," said Mindy as she gathered some seaweed strands.

"What do we do, Mindy?" asked Patrick.

"Ummm . . . spin around three times," she instructed.

They did.

"I think it's working," said SpongeBob.

"Good . . . now keep your eyes shut."

As she talked she bundled the seaweed together.

"The mermaid's magic," said Mindy. "With my one tail fin, I command the two of you to turn into men."

She placed a bundle of seaweed on SpongeBob's face, then on Patrick's. The seaweed looked just like bushy mustaches.

"Open your eyes!" she told them.

They did.

"Goodness gracious, Patrick!" cried SpongeBob, pointing to Patrick's face. "You have a mustache!"

"So do you!" said Patrick.

They marveled at their new mustaches!

"Okay," said Mindy, snapping them back to

reality. "Now that you're men, can you make it to Shell City?"

But SpongeBob and Patrick were still in mustache heaven.

"Guys!" she called.

"Eh?" said SpongeBob, still twirling his mustache.

"I said, now that you're men, can you make it to Shell City?"

"Heck yeah," SpongeBob told her.

"And are men afraid of anything?" asked Mindy.

"Heck no!" cried SpongeBob and Patrick.

"And why is that?" she asked.

SpongeBob and Patrick pumped their fists in the air. "Because we're invincible!" they shouted.

Then SpongeBob and Patrick raced to the cliff's edge and jumped!

"I never said *that*!" Mindy cried.

But it was too late.

She ran to the trench and looked in. They'd already been swallowed up by the darkness. But she could hear them cheering all the way down.

CHAPTER 11

SpongeBob and Patrick were falling! But they didn't care. They had their mustaches. All was right with the world.

"Yeah!" cried SpongeBob, flapping his arms.

"Heeeee-yah!" Patrick screamed, spinning end over end.

They fell and fell and fell. Soon the thrill was gone. And the fear came over them.

"Uh, Pat?" said SpongeBob.

"Yeah?"

"Why did we jump over the edge instead of taking the stairs?" asked SpongeBob.

"Because . . . ah . . . well . . . huh," Patrick replied.

Finally they looked down. The bottom was

rushing up to meet them—really, really fast! They hugged each other, closed their eyes, and screamed.

Then they hit a branch. And another. And another. Each branch broke their fall a little so when they finally landed, it wasn't so bad.

"Patrick, we're alive!" cried SpongeBob.

"Wow," said Patrick, amazed. "The mustaches work!"

SpongeBob whooped. "You know what this means? We *are* invincible!"

With that, the boys started to sing as they marched deeper into the mysterious trench.

They marched on as if nothing could stand in their way.

As they sang, a monster Gobble Fish opened its mouth and swallowed SpongeBob and Patrick whole. But the new men weren't fazed. They just kept on marching right through the monster and out the other end, twiddling their new mustaches.

As they sang, Patrick and SpongeBob dodged doom. Monster clam traps tried to grab hold of the men. But they just hopped in and out of them. A deadly Manta Monster swooped down to attack, but SpongeBob was twirling his mustache so fast that the creature got confused and slammed into a rock!

Patrick skipped through a patch of stinging jellyfish. The jellyfish were so surprised, they ended up stinging *one another*! Now that Mindy made them men, nothing and no one could stand in their way.

Giant sharks and snapping great sponge- and starfish-eating sea turtles were no match for SpongeBob and Patrick. They danced over shark snouts and used the turtles' shells for surfboards! The men were having the time of their lives.

Enormous fish surrounded the two men. Everywhere they turned, SpongeBob and Patrick were faced with the scariest predators they had ever seen. But when they broke into their amazing tap-dance routine, the monster fish were amazed and awed.

Finally, the monsters realized there was no use in trying to eat SpongeBob and Patrick now that they were men. Instead, they joined in the festivities. Soon the whole trench was singing and dancing. The biggest, meanest monsters joined in the song and picked up SpongeBob and Patrick in celebration. Now that they were men, the monsters became their friends and rooted them on as they went to save the crown.

"We did it, Pat," said SpongeBob. "We made it past all the hideous disgusting monsters."

When the monster fish overheard SpongeBob, they all gasped. Their feelings were hurt, so they quickly swam back to their trench.

"Not you guys!" SpongeBob called. "You guys are awesome!"

Then SpongeBob flashed them a big thumbs-up.

But it was too late. The monster fish had already swum back down into their deep, dark trench.

"Oh, well," SpongeBob said, watching his monster pals go.

Then he slapped Patrick on the back. "Time's a wastin'. We gotta get the crown and save the town and Mr. Krabs. Woo-hoo!

"Come on, Pat," said SpongeBob, taking his hand and leading him away. "Let's get the crown."

Patrick and SpongeBob traveled for days. They journeyed over rivers and through valleys, along reefs and through jungles of seaweed.

SpongeBob and Patrick slept in shallow water, under the twinkling stars. They ran with a herd of wild sea horses. They ate lunch with a pack of sea cucumbers.

Finally they came to a sign that read SHELL CITY, DEAD AHEAD.

"Woooooo!" cheered SpongeBob and Patrick.

SpongeBob pulled out his calendar and tore off the top page. *Rrrrrrrrrip!*

Ouch, that's gotta hurt, SpongeBob thought to himself. "Sorry about that, calendar," he whispered.

Then SpongeBob turned to Patrick and pointed to the date.

"Pat! This is great," he said. "We're going to make it to Shell City with an extra day to spare! I think we'll even have time to get something to eat."

"Finally I got you right where I want you," said a gruff voice.

The two friends turned. There was Dennis. He was sitting on his motorcycle and cracking his knuckles.

"Who are you?" asked SpongeBob.

"Name's Dennis," he said, touching the brim of his cowboy hat. "I was hired to whup you."

"He's gonna get us!" SpongeBob cried fearfully.

Then he laughed. So did Patrick. They laughed and laughed until they were blue. Finally SpongeBob caught his breath. Dennis was not amused.

"Listen, stranger," SpongeBob said. "I don't know who you're working for, but I'm gonna do you a little favor. Obviously you don't know who you're dealing with here, so if you'll just step aside, we'll forget this whole thing."

But Dennis just cracked another knuckle. "Oh, you'll forget the whole thing, all right, once I get you!"

SpongeBob's eyes narrowed.

"Well," he said, "we tried to warn you, pencil-neck. Now it's time to feel the wrath of our mustaches!"

Dennis reached out and grabbed the seaweed

under their noses and ripped it off!

"You mean these?" he said. "I thought you still had a piece of salad stuck to your lip from lunchtime."

"Th-they were fake?" SpongeBob stammered.

"Of course they were fake," said Dennis. "This is what a real mustache looks like!"

Dennis clenched his face until he turned purple. Suddenly a bushy mustache pushed through the skin over his upper lip.

Patrick and SpongeBob were impressed.

"Is he a mermaid?" asked Patrick.

"All right, enough gab!" snapped Dennis.

"What . . . are you gonna do to us?" SpongeBob asked anxiously.

"Plankton was very specific," said Dennis. "For some reason, he wants me to step on you. That way you'll never find out that he stole the crown. . . . Uh, perhaps I've said too much."

Dennis lifted his boot, and long spikes popped out. He held his foot over them as they stood trembling with fear.

"That's a big boot!" cried Patrick.

"Don't worry," said Dennis. "This'll only hurt a lot." He laughed and laughed. "I love this job!"

But just as Dennis was about to stomp on SpongeBob and Patrick, something appeared behind him. Then a humongous giant boot squashed Dennis flat.

Patrick looked up and screamed, "Bigger boot!"

CHAPTER 12

A giant shadow fell over them.

Patrick and SpongeBob gazed with awe at the bigger boot. Then Patrick got *really* scared, so scared that he wanted to run away, but SpongeBob held him back.

"Wait, Pat. This bigger boot saved our lives."

They looked up and saw the owner of the boot— a giant standing over them.

"Thank you, stranger," Patrick said politely.

The scary giant did not reply. But he *did* move closer and was now towering over SpongeBob and Patrick. The giant had a big metal head with bubbles coming out of it. He was looking down at them with one eye. One eye? ONE EYE!

"It's the Cyclops! RUUUUUUN!"

SpongeBob and Patrick ran. But it was too late. With his big boots clomping on the ground, the Cyclops ran the boys down and swooped them up in his colossal hands.

"AHHHHHHHHHH!" the boys screamed as the Cyclops stuffed them into a dark and scary bag.

The Cyclops swam to a boat and climbed aboard. Then he opened his underwater bag and peeked inside.

SpongeBob and Patrick had fainted, so the Cyclops tossed the sponge and the starfish into a bowl filled with water.

Then he started his boat and headed toward the shore.

❖❖❖❖❖❖❖

SpongeBob and Patrick awoke on a lumpy bed of pink, red, blue, and yellow rocks.

"Huh?" SpongeBob grunted, rubbing his head.

"Are we dead?" asked Patrick.

SpongeBob looked around. "I don't think so."

He checked out the scenery, which was pretty

strange. "Hey, artificially colored rocks!"

Patrick ate one. "Mmm, strawberry . . ."

SpongeBob got up and stretched. "Well, let's go, Patrick. I don't know where we are but—"

BUMP!

"Oops! What's this?" SpongeBob had walked into an invisible glass wall.

"Ooooh. It's some kind of wall of psychic energy," said Patrick.

But SpongeBob shook his head. It was worse than that! "No, Patrick. It's a giant glass bowl. We're in a fishbowl!"

SpongeBob looked around. He was relieved to see they were not alone. "Hey, there's some fish folk over there."

In fact the place had more fish folk than a Goofy Goober's Party Boat on its busiest night! There were fish all over the place.

"Hey! Over here," called SpongeBob, waving.

"Hey!" cried Patrick, jumping up and down.

But the fish just stared straight ahead, ignoring them.

"Hey, you guys? Help!"

"Yeah," said SpongeBob. "A little help here. We're stuck in this—"

Then SpongeBob's eyes bugged out.

"Over here!" called Patrick, still trying to get the fish folk's attention.

"Wait a second!" said SpongeBob. "Those fish! They're all . . . all . . . all *dried up*!"

"AAAAHHHHH," yelled Patrick.

"AAAARGHHHH," yelled SpongeBob.

Then they heard a deep, booming laugh that shook the walls of their prison. The Cyclops! A giant human dressed in a diving suit was staring right into their bowl.

"What's he gonna do with us?" cried SpongeBob.

They watched as the giant took a bottle of glue out of his toolbox.

"OH, NO!" yelled SpongeBob, trembling. "He's going for his evil instruments of torture."

The Cyclops set the glue on a table next to a bottle of plastic googly eyes.

"Glue?" shrieked SpongeBob. "Googly eyes? Ahhhhhhh!"

As they watched with dread, the giant glued a pair of googly eyes onto a dried-up clam. Then he put a hat on the clam's head and a tiny plastic phone in the little dried-up guy's hand.

SpongeBob gasped. "He's making a humorous diorama out of that poor clam!"

Finally the giant hung a little paper sign around the clam's neck that read—

"Alexander Clam Bell?!"

Poor SpongeBob couldn't believe his eyes.

"Patrick, he's drying up sea animals and making them into smelly knickknacks!"

"And we're next!" screamed Patrick.

At that moment the giant reached into the fish bowl and grabbed Patrick.

"Paaaaaaaatrick!"

Then another hand reached in and clutched SpongeBob.

"Nooooooo!"

The giant dropped them onto a table, right under

a bright, hot light. Instantly Patrick and SpongeBob started to sizzle in the heat.

"The heat from this lamp is so intense, I can't move," SpongeBob said weakly.

"Tell me about it," said Patrick, practically parched.

They heard the Cyclops laugh and stomp away, but still they could not escape. The heat from the light was drying them out. They were growing weaker by the minute.

"This doesn't look too good, Patrick," said SpongeBob.

"You mean we're not gonna . . . get the crown, save the town, Mr. Krabs. . . ." Patrick sang softly, his voice fading.

"I don't even think we're going to be able to save ourselves, buddy," SpongeBob said, gasping.

He tried to wipe his forehead, but his arm was so brittle it broke off!

Patrick rolled to his side and put it back on for his pal.

"Thanks," SpongeBob wheezed.

"Don't mention it." Patrick coughed.

"Well," said SpongeBob, "it looks like what everyone said was true."

Patrick managed to smile. "You mean that we're attractive?"

"No," said SpongeBob as tiny cracks appeared on his skin. "That we're just kids—a couple of kids way over our heads. We were doomed from the start. I mean, look at us—we didn't even come close to the crown. We let everybody down. We failed."

Patrick's eyes bugged out. "Shell City?"

"Yeah." SpongeBob sighed sadly. "We never made it to Shell City."

"Shell City," said Patrick.

"Exactly, buddy," said SpongeBob. "That's the place we never got to."

"Shell City!" Patrick cried.

"Okay, now you're starting to bum me out, Patrick."

"No," said Patrick, pointing. "Look at the sign! Shell City—Marine Gifts and Sundry."

SpongeBob gasped. "Shell City's a gift shop? But,

if this is Shell City, then where's the . . . ?"

SpongeBob and Patrick saw it at the same time.

"THE CROWN!" cried SpongeBob and Patrick.
It was dazzling in the sunlight.

"Neptune's crown!" yelled SpongeBob. "This *is*
Shell City!"

By this time they had almost no strength left.
In seconds they would be completely dry. But still
Patrick and SpongeBob felt proud.

"Pat, we *did* make it," said SpongeBob, a smile
crossing his cracking and drying face.

"Yeah," Patrick said, sniffling. "I guess we did."

"We did all right for a couple of goofballs,"
SpongeBob said with a sigh, shedding a single tear.
Then he started to sing softly.

"I'm a Goofy Goober, yeah . . ."

"You're a Goofy Goober, yeah," sang Patrick,
shedding a tear too.

"We're all Goofy Goobers, yeah," they sang
together. "Goofy, Goofy, Goober, Goober . . ."

Then they closed their eyes and dried up.

But all was not lost, for the tears they shed joined

together to form a single drop of water. And that drop of water flowed off the table, down the lamp's wire, and into the electric socket.

The lamp shorted out. A mighty shower of sparks left the smoke rising to the ceiling of the Shell City gift shop. The sprinklers sprang open.

Water rained down on everything in the store— including SpongeBob and Patrick. Their bodies soaked up the water, and in no time the two Goofy Goobers woke up!

"Hey, we're alive!" exclaimed SpongeBob, looking down at his hands, just as soft and spongy as ever. "Let's get that crown!"

"Right!"

The boys jumped down and ran across the wet floor. Water was still pouring down from the sprinklers. The boys made it to the crown and tried to lift it.

"On three, Pat. Are you ready?" cried SpongeBob. "One . . . two . . . three!"

The crown flew into the air, with SpongeBob and Patrick still hanging on.

SpongeBob was surprised. "It's lighter than I thought!"

Then he realized that his feet weren't touching the ground. SpongeBob blinked, and when he opened his eyes again, he was staring into the face of the Cyclops.

"AHHHHHHH!"

The giant was holding the crown in his enormous hand. When he saw SpongeBob and Patrick hanging there, he roared with anger.

CHAPTER 13

The Cyclops was really mad. Two stupid sea animals had wrecked his shop. He was ready to squash SpongeBob and Patrick when he heard a terrible sound.

He looked up, then screamed.

All of the sea animals he had dried up were alive again—and they were really, really mad!

The puffer fish puffed up and charged the giant, sticking him with their little points. Sea horses neighed and stampeded over the giant's toes. The clown fish attacked his shins. And the mariachi fish played their music—a song that spelled doom for the cruel one-eyed monster who had tortured them!

A lobster squirted glue into the Cyclops's eye and he squealed. Clams snapped at his butt and he yelped.

Then all the fish cheered as the giant slipped on the water and fell down. With claws snapping, teeth gnashing, and fins finning, the fish closed in on the evil Cyclops.

"Come on, Patrick!" yelled SpongeBob.

They both grabbed the crown and ran to the dock.

"You still have that bag of winds?" SpongeBob asked.

"Sure do!" said Patrick.

"Okay, let's go over the instructions," said SpongeBob as he unfolded them.

He began to read: "Step one. Point bag away from home."

"Okay," said Patrick, pointing the bag away from Bikini Bottom.

"Step two: Plant feet firmly on the ground."

"Right," said Patrick, his feet planted.

"Step three," SpongeBob read. "Remove string from bag, releasing winds."

"Check," said Patrick as he pulled the string.

With a whoosh the winds rushed out of the bag.

The force snapped the sack out of Patrick's hand and it sailed away like a balloon full of air!

Patrick stared at his empty hands in surprise.

"Well, that sounds simple enough," said SpongeBob, still clueless about what had just happened. "Point the bag away from home, feet firmly on ground, pull string releasing the winds."

SpongeBob tucked the instructions into his pocket.

"All right," he said, rubbing his hands together. "Let's do it for real."

"Uh, SpongeBob?" said Patrick sheepishly.

SpongeBob turned around and Patrick pointed toward the bag.

There was the bag of winds, hurling through the sky far out to sea. It was heading toward Bikini Bottom and home—without them!

"Oh, no!" cried SpongeBob. "How will we ever get back to Bikini Bottom now?"

"I can take you there," said a friendly voice.

SpongeBob and Patrick looked up to see a man running toward them across a white sandy beach.

The man's head was a mass of black curls. His face rugged and tanned, muscles hard and rippling. He wore a bright red swimsuit and carried a flotation device. And his smile was brighter than the California sun.

"What are you?" said SpongeBob.

"I'm a lifeguard," the man in the red swimsuit replied.

Patrick and SpongeBob whooped. *Saved!*

"So where's your boat?" asked SpongeBob.

The lifeguard threw back his handsome head and laughed. His teeth were white and pearly.

"Boat?" he said. "Who needs a boat?"

With that, he tossed SpongeBob, Patrick, and Neptune's crown on his broad back and jumped into the water.

"Go!" cheered SpongeBob.

With mighty strokes the buff lifeguard swam like a torpedo toward Bikini Bottom, where . . .

❖❖❖❖❖❖❖❖

The evil Plankton was taunting poor, frozen Mr. Krabs.

"Well, Krabs," cooed Plankton. "You know what today is?"

The mad ruler of Planktopolis ripped a page from the calendar and cruelly tossed it into a wastebasket.

"Why, it's March fourteenth. But wait! That's not right." Plankton chuckled. "It *should* say 'the day that Krabs gets punished!' Ha, ha, ha, ha, ha!"

Just then a fanfare played and in walked the squire.

"Presenting old iron fist himself . . . King Neptune!"

Neptune's trident reached through the door and bopped the squire on the head. Then King Neptune entered the Krusty Krab 2 in all his regal glory.

"Greetings, sire," said Plankton with a bow. "Glad you could make it. I got the crab set up here for ya!"

Inside the ice, Mr. Krabs shivered.

Plankton pulled up a chair and said, "I'm all ready on my end."

"Who are you?" King Neptune demanded.

"Me?" said Plankton with a phony smile. "Oh,

I'm just a concerned citizen waiting to see justice done. This crab must pay for his horrible crimes."

Then the evil Plankton eyed Mr. Krabs. "Might I suggest aiming for his head, Your Highness?"

◆◆◆◆◆◆◆◆◆

Meanwhile the lifeguard was cutting through the ocean waves like a speedboat. As he swam, he passed a fisherman's dinghy. The incredible force of his wake rocked the boat and threw the fisherman into the water.

SpongeBob and Patrick hung on as they raced for home. Up ahead they spied a familiar green island.

"Hooray for the lifeguard!" cheered SpongeBob. "Nothing can stop us now!"

"Uh-oh," cried Patrick. "Unidentified object off the hindquarters."

As the boys watched, a giant boot rose out of the ocean and was gaining on them. The Cyclops's boot!

"Bigger boot?" said SpongeBob. "But how?"

A powerful gust of wind blew the boot away. Underneath it was Dennis with a mean grin on his face.

"Did ya miss me?"

"AHHHHHH! It's Dennis!" yelled SpongeBob.

⬥⬥⬥⬥⬥⬥⬥⬥⬥

Back inside the Krusty Krab 2, a fish drummed a sad tune as King Neptune prepared to punish Mr. Krabs.

Plankton ate marshmallows and enjoyed the exciting show.

"This is the best seat in the house!" Plankton gushed. "All right, King Neptune, let's get it on."

King Neptune rose up to his full kingly height. He aimed his trident at Mr. Krabs.

"Eugene Krabs," said the king. "Your six-day reprieve is up and it is time for your punishment."

A tear rolled down Mr. Krabs's chilly cheek.

"I'm sorry, but there is nothing else I can do," said the king.

Princess Mindy appeared at her father's side.

"You can give SpongeBob and Patrick a little more time."

"What? Mindy!" King Neptune bellowed angrily.

"Will you butt out! I'm tired of you trying to stall this crab's punishment."

"Stalling," said Mindy, wounded. "Why, I'm not stalling anything."

"Yes, you are."

"No, I'm not."

"Yes, you are," roared the king. "You're doing it right now."

"Doing what?"

"Stalling!" cried King Neptune.

"No, I am not," Mindy insisted.

"Yes, you are!"

"No."

"Yes."

Plankton shook his head and sighed. "Oh, boy," he muttered. The evil leader of Planktopolis was losing patience with this pair.

◆◇◆◇◆◇◆

On board the lifeguard's back, things were not going well for Patrick and SpongeBob.

"Now," said Dennis, his shadow looming over them. "Where were we?"

"Patrick, run!"

But Patrick stood his ground—or rather, the lifeguard's back.

"No," he said. "I'm tired of running. If we run now, we'll never stop."

Patrick cracked his knuckles and looked up at Dennis. The biker hauled off and whacked the little starfish. Patrick flew through the air and landed on the lifeguard's foot, where he held on for dear life.

"Run, SpongeBob!" yelled Patrick.

SpongeBob ran down the lifeguard's back, across his butt, and down his leg. Dennis was right behind him. The evil biker extended the spikes in his boots and ran across the deck—or rather, the lifeguard's back.

"Hey! Take it easy back there, fellows," cried the lifeguard.

Dennis came closer and closer. The spikes in his boots were gleaming.

"Come on, kid, give it up," said Dennis. "I always get my man."

SpongeBob was trapped. He looked down at the

ocean waves churning between the lifeguard's mighty legs. Then he took a deep breath.

"I'll never give up!" the plucky sponge cried as he jumped from one leg to the other.

"Yay!" crowed SpongeBob. "I made it!"

But so did Dennis. "You've got guts, kid. Too bad I got to rip 'em outta ya."

"Look," said SpongeBob. "I don't know what Plankton's paying you. But if you let us go, I promise I can make it worth your while."

SpongeBob reached into the pocket of his pants and pulled out a wad of bills. He stuffed them into Dennis's hand.

"It's gonna take a lot more than . . ." Dennis looked at the bills. "Hey, what is this anyway?"

"That, sir, is five goober dollars," SpongeBob told him. "Legal tender at any participating Goofy Goober's Party Boat location."

Dennis grabbed SpongeBob by the throat.

"I've got bubbles. Fun at parties," said the desperate SpongeBob, blowing a few. The bubbles rushed toward Dennis and burst in his face.

"Uhhhhh," he screamed. "My eyes! I've got soap bubbles in my eyes!"

Dennis tossed SpongeBob over the side. He landed in the water, but as SpongeBob floated by, Patrick caught him.

"I've got you," said the brave little starfish.

SpongeBob climbed aboard the lifeguard's foot until he was next to Patrick, clinging to the heel.

"Thanks, buddy," SpongeBob said.

Then Dennis appeared, standing over them. His spiked boot was raised over their heads, ready to stomp them flat.

"I'm through messing around. See you later, fools," he said.

Just then the lifeguard swam beneath an oncoming catamaran and knocked Dennis into the sea.

"See ya," said Patrick, waving.

CHAPTER 14

Meanwhile, back in Bikini Bottom—er, the Evil Empire of Planktopolis—Mindy and King Neptune were still arguing.

"No, I'm not," said Mindy.

"Yes, you are," said the king.

"No, I'm not," said Mindy.

King Neptune grabbed his head and tore at his hair.

"Aaaaahhhh!" Neptune roared. "Where am I? In crazy town? I've had enough of this nonsense. Mindy, you are to wait in the carriage until the execution is done."

"But, Daddy—"

"NOW!"

Thunder and lightning flashed and the trident crackled with energy. Mindy scurried outside as fast as she could. As she went, Plankton stuck his tongue out at her.

To be extra sure that the princess wouldn't give them any more trouble, Neptune fired a blast from his magic trident. Chains and padlocks appeared, sealing the doors and windows.

"Ha, ha, ha!" chuckled Plankton.

Outside, Mindy banged on the doors.

"Oh, SpongeBob," she said quietly to herself. "Wherever you are, you'd better hurry!"

◆◆◆◆◆◆◆◆◆◆

The lifeguard was swimming past a familiar island. He looked over his broad shoulders at his passengers.

"Okay, fellas, this is where you get off. Bikini Bottom is directly below."

"But we'll never be able to float down in time," cried SpongeBob, looking at his calendar.

The lifeguard smiled. It was as dazzling as King Neptune's shiny head. "Who said anything about floating?"

With that, he flexed his muscular chest.

SpongeBob's mouth gaped. Patrick's eyes were wide.

"Did you see that, Pat?"

"What control!" Patrick marveled.

The lifeguard grabbed the crown—with SpongeBob and Patrick hanging on.

"All hands on deck!" he said. Then he placed the crown, along with SpongeBob and Patrick, between his muscular pecs.

"Hang on, Pat!" cried SpongeBob.

"What choice do I have?"

❖❖❖❖❖❖❖❖

Far below, in the heart of Planktopolis, Mr. Krabs was about to be punished.

"Eugene Krabs," said King Neptune as he warmed up his trident.

"No," Mindy gasped as she watched helplessly through the window.

"Yes!" cried Plankton, mad eyes gleaming.

"The time has come—," said the king. The tip of his staff sparkled with energy.

"No!" said Mindy.

"Yes . . . ," hissed Plankton.

"—for your—"

"No!" screamed Mindy.

"Yes!" howled Plankton.

"—*punishment.*"

Bolts of thunder leaped from the trident. The air in the Krusty Krab 2 crackled with power.

◆◆◆◆◆◆◆◆◆◆◆

Meanwhile, on the ocean's surface, the lifeguard was ready to launch torpedoes!

With one last, mighty squeeze, the crown, SpongeBob, and Patrick were fired into the ocean's watery depths. Spinning wildly, and giving SpongeBob and Patrick the ride of their lives, the crown plunged toward the Krusty Krab 2. The crown smashed through the roof. Down came SpongeBob and Patrick!

And as Neptune fired his blast, SpongeBob held up the crown and deflected the bolt with its shiny surface. Mr. Krabs was saved!

"My crown . . . ," Neptune said as he picked up

his crown and held it close to his chest. "My *beautiful* crown!"

Just then Mindy came flying through the double doors.

"SpongeBob! Patrick!" Mindy cried, clapping. "I knew you could do it!"

"Oh, yes, well done, SpongeBoob," added Plankton in a mocking tone.

"Sorry to rain on your parade, Plankton," said SpongeBob.

"Oh, don't worry about me, my parade shall be quite dry—under my umbrella," replied Plankton, yanking down on a chord dangling from above.

"An umbrella?" said SpongeBob, baffled. "Huh?"

A trapdoor in the ceiling swung open, and a chum bucket fell right onto King Neptune's head.

"Daddy, no!" cried Mindy.

But the helmet was humming and Neptune's brain had already gone numb.

"Daddy, yes!" said Plankton, whipping out a

remote control and pushing down on its big button. Responding to the signal from the remote, an antenna rose up from Neptune's helmet, and Neptune quickly stiffened.

"All hail Plankton," mumbled Neptune.

"Ahhhh!" cried SpongeBob, Patrick, and Mindy in unison.

Suddenly all the bucket-headed fish smashed through the windows of the restaurant. Quickly they surrounded SpongeBob, Patrick, Mindy, and the frozen Mr. Krabs, leaving them with no place to go!

On command from Plankton, Neptune fired up his trident.

"SpongeBob, what happened?" asked Patrick.

"Plankton cheated," said SpongeBob.

"Cheated?" said Plankton, jumping off one of the tables and walking over to SpongeBob and Patrick. He turned and raised a hand back in Neptune's direction. "Hold on, baldy."

On Plankton's command Neptune remained still.

"Oh, grow up. What do you think this is—a

game of kickball on the playground? You never had a chance to defeat me, fool. And do you know why?" asked Plankton.

"Because you cheated?" responded SpongeBob.

"No, not because I cheated. Because I'm an evil genius and you're just a kid—a stupid kid! Ah, ha, ha, ha!" said Plankton as he burst into a maniacal laugh.

King Neptune and the bucket-headed fish joined Plankton, filling the Krusty Krab 2 with a booming laughter.

SpongeBob slouched. "I guess you're right, Plankton," he said, looking defeated. "I am just a kid."

"Of course I'm right," said Plankton. "Okay, Neptune, time to—"

"And you know," continued SpongeBob, "I've been through a lot in the last six days, five minutes, twenty-seven and a half seconds. And if I've learned anything during that time it is that you are who you are."

"That's right," replied Plankton. "Okay, Neptune, would you—"

But SpongeBob kept on talking.

"And no amount of mermaid magic—"

SpongeBob pointed to Mindy.

"—or managerial promotion—"

He pointed toward Mr. Krabs.

"—or some other third thing can make me anything more than what I really am inside—a *kid*."

"All right! That's great!" cried an antsy Plankton. "Now back against the wall!"

Just then a microphone dropped into SpongeBob's hands.

"But that's okay!" shouted SpongeBob into the microphone. "Because I did what everyone said a kid couldn't do. I *made* it to Shell City, I *beat* the Cyclops, and I brought back the crown!"

"All right, we get the point," Plankton moaned, now beating his head against the wall.

"So yeah, I'm a kid!" cried SpongeBob. "And I'm also a goofball! And a wing nut! And a Knucklehead McSpazatron!"

Smoke started to rise from the floor, and a spotlight was now shining on SpongeBob.

"But most of all, I'm . . . I'm . . . I'm . . ."

Eyes wide, everyone waited for SpongeBob to tell the world what he truly was.

(Please see the next page.)

CHAPTER 15

Standing in the middle of the spotlight, SpongeBob jumped up. Suddenly he was wearing sunglasses and sporting a heavy-metal attitude.

"I'm a Goofy Goober!" SpongeBob sang as a guitar appeared in his hands.

The force of his riff sent Plankton flying backward. The evil genius crashed into Karen the Computer's screen and stuck there like chewing gum.

"You're a Goofy Goober!" roared SpongeBob in Plankton's face. "We're *all* Goofy Goobers!"

"What's he doing?" Plankton asked.

"GOOFY, GOOFY, GOOFY, GOOFY GOOBER!" sang SpongeBob, bringing down the house and sending the bucket-headed fish army spinning away.

"Enough already!" yelled Plankton.

But SpongeBob just kept on singing.

"What's going on?" Plankton cried anxiously. "This isn't right. Karen?"

But Karen the Computer was singing along too. "You have to admit it's catchy," she said.

SpongeBob did the worm—backward—across the floor, still strumming his electric riffs.

He stuck out his tongue and pumped his fist in the air.

"I'm a Goofy Goober!"

Plankton turned to his army of bucket-heads.

"Seize him!" he cried.

But SpongeBob's music was overpowering. Suddenly, one by one, the helmets broke off. Horrified, Plankton watched as SpongeBob freed his bucket-headed army.

"Noooooooooooo!" Plankton yelled. "His chops are too righteous. The helmets can't handle this level of rock 'n' roll. Karen . . . do something!"

By this time Karen the Computer had also succumbed to SpongeBob's music, and Plankton looked up only to find her crowd surfing.

"All right," cried Plankton. "That's the last straw. Neptune, I command you to—"

But Plankton was too late. SpongeBob's music had already set Neptune free.

"I better get out of here!" Plankton muttered to himself, heading toward the entrance of the Krusty Krab 2. As he reached the front door it burst open and a flood of freed fish swarmed into the restaurant, stampeding over Plankton.

"Owwwwwwwwwwww!"

CHAPTER 16

A few hours later things were back to normal in Bikini Bottom—more or less.

Plankton was locked up in a police truck, heading for a special place: the Institution for the Criminally Tiny. He was clinging to the bars of the truck, trying to talk himself out of trouble.

"Aww, come on," Plankton said. "I was just kidding. Come on, you knew that . . . didn't you? With the helmets? And the big monument? Wasn't that hilarious, everybody?"

SpongeBob, Patrick, and Princess Mindy watched as the truck drove away.

"I'll get even with all of you!" Plankton yelled. And then he was gone, like a bad scoop of ice cream in the hot summer sun.

Inside the wrecked Krusty Krab 2, Neptune was waiting for them.

"Well, Mindy," the king said, "I have to admit you were right. Your compassion for these sea creatures proved a most admirable trait. Without it I would never again have seen my beloved crown."

He smiled down at his daughter. "Now, let's go home."

"Daddy, haven't you forgotten something?" asked Mindy.

"What? Oh, yes," Neptune said. "Eugene Krabs, I unfreeze you."

He fired his trident and Mr. Krabs was unfrozen—and was turned into a fat little boy.

"Oops!" Neptune cried. "I guess I had it set to 'Real Boy Ending.'"

Embarrassed, Neptune fiddled with his trident. Then he fired again.

"Yipes!" yelled Mr. Krabs, and just like that he was back to his old self.

"I'm sorry for falsely freezing you, Krabs," said

Neptune. "And may I say, sir, that you are very lucky to have in your employ such a brave, faithful, and heroic young lad."

SpongeBob beamed with pride.

King Neptune prodded Krabs with his trident.

"Go to him now," said the monarch of the sea. "Embrace the lad."

"SpongeBob, my boy," said Mr. Krabs, "I'm sorry I ever doubted ya. That's a mistake I won't ever make again."

"Aw, Mr. Krabs, you old soft-serve," said SpongeBob, blushing.

"And now, SpongeBob, I'm going to do something that I should have done six days ago. Mr. Squidward, front and center please," ordered Mr. Krabs. "I think we all know who deserves to rightfully wear that manager pin."

"I couldn't agree with you more, sir," said Squidward, forcing a smile as he reluctantly removed his pin.

The residents of Bikini Bottom burst into cheer. "Hooray for SpongeBob!"

"Wait a second, everybody," said SpongeBob in a serious tone.

"I think I know what it is," said Squidward. "After going on your life-changing journey, you now realize you don't want what you thought you wanted."

Squidward put an arm on SpongeBob's shoulder and continued. "What you really wanted was inside you all along."

"Are you crazy?" cried SpongeBob, snatching the pin from Squidward. "I was just going to tell you that your fly is down."

SpongeBob put on the pin, and with a huge grin he cried out, "Manager! This is the greatest day of my life!"